DEAD OVER HEELS

AN AURORA TEAGARDEN MYSTERY

CHARLAINE HARRIS

An Orion paperback

First published in Great Britain in 2010
by Gollancz
This paperback edition published in 2013
by Orion Books,
an imprint of The Orion Publishing Group Ltd,
Orion House, 5 Upper St Martin's Lane,
London WC2H 9EA

An Hachette UK company

1 3 5 7 9 10 8 6 4 2

A CIP catalogue record for this book
is available from the British Library.

ISBN 978-1-4091-4714-5

Typeset at The Spartan Press Ltd,
Lymington, Hants

Printed and bound in Great Britain by
Clays Ltd, St Ives plc

The Orion Publishing Group's policy is to use papers
that are natural, renewable and recyclable products and
made from wood grown in sustainable forests. The logging
and manufacturing processes are expected to conform to
the environmental regulations of the country of origin.

www.charlaineharris.com
www.orionbooks.co.uk

04882835

Charlaine Harris is the bestselling author of the *Sookie Stackhouse* series, adapted for HBO as *True Blood*, as well as three other exceptional series – *The Aurora Teagarden Mysteries*, *The Lily Bard Mysteries* and *The Harper Connelly Series*. She is married, with children, and lives in central Texas.

By Charlaine Harris

STANDALONE NOVELS

Sweet and Deadly
A Secret Rage

THE AURORA TEAGARDEN MYSTERIES

Real Murders
A Bone to Pick
Three Bedrooms, One Corpse
The Julius House
Dead Over Heels
A Fool and His Honey
Last Scene Alive
Poppy Done to Death

THE LILY BARD MYSTERIES

Shakespeare's Landlord
Shakespeare's Champion
Shakespeare's Christmas
Shakespeare's Trollop
Shakespeare's Counselor

THE SOOKIE STACKHOUSE NOVELS

Dead Until Dark
Living Dead in Dallas
Club Dead
Dead to the World
Dead as a Doornail
Definitely Dead
All Together Dead
From Dead to Worse
Dead and Gone
Dead in the Family
Dead Reckoning
Deadlocked
Dead Ever After
A Touch of Dead
The Sookie Stackhouse
   Companion

THE HARPER CONNELLY SERIES

Grave Sight
Grave Surprise
An Ice Cold Grave
Grave Secret

For my agent, Joshua Bilmes

Chapter One

My bodyguard was mowing the yard wearing her pink bikini when the man fell from the sky.

I was occupied with adjusting the angle of the back of my folding 'lounger', which I'd erected with some difficulty on the patio.

I had some warning, since I'd been aware of the buzzing of the plane for several seconds while I struggled to get the back of the lounger to settle somewhere between totally prone and rigidly upright. But Angel had one of those little tape players strapped to her waist (the plastic belt looked strange with the bikini) and the headphones and the drone of the lawn mower made her oblivious to the unusual persistence of the noise.

Circling low, I thought with some annoyance. I figured an aviator had spotted Angel and was making the most of his lucky day. Meantime, the ice in my coffee was melting and my book was lying on the little lawn table unread, while I wrestled with the stupid chair. Finally succeeding in locking the back of the lounger into a position approximating comfort, I looked up just in time to see something large falling from the little plane, something that rotated horribly, head over heels.

My gut recognized disaster seconds before my civilized self (which was pretty much just saying 'Huh?') and propelled me off the patio and across the yard to knock Angel, all five feet eleven of her, away from the handle of the mower and under the shelter of an oak tree.

A sickening thud followed immediately.

In the ensuing silence, I could hear the plane buzzing away.

'What the *hell* was that?' Angel gasped. Her headphones had been knocked off, so she'd heard the impact. I was half on top of her; it must have looked as if a Chihuahua was frolicking with a Great Dane. I turned my head to look, dreading what I would see.

Luckily, he'd landed face down.

Even so, I was nearly sick on our newly mown grass, and Angel quite definitely was.

'I don't know why you had to knock me down,' Angel said in a voice distinctly different from her flat south Florida drawl. 'He probably missed me by, oh, thirteen inches.'

We were pushing ourselves to our feet, moving carefully.

'I didn't want to have to buy a new lawn mower,' I said through clenched teeth. A side chamber in my mind was feeling grateful that our lawn mower was one of those that stop moving when the handle is released.

Angel was right about it being a man, judging from the clothes and the haircut. He was wearing a purple-and-white check shirt and brown pants, but the fashion police were not going to be bothering him anymore. A very little blood stained the shirt as I looked. He'd landed spread-eagled; one leg stuck out at a very unalive angle. And then there was the way his neck was turned . . . I looked away hastily and took some long, deep breaths.

'He must be three inches into the ground,' Angel observed, still in that shaky voice.

She seemed preoccupied with measurements today.

Paralyzed by the suddenness and totality of the disaster, we stood together in the shade of the oak, looking at the body lying in the sun. Neither of us approached it. There was a stain spreading through the grass and dirt in the head area.

'And of course, the guys aren't here today,' I said bitterly, apropos of nothing. 'They're never home when you need them.' Angel looked at me, her jaw dropping. Then she began hooting with laughter.

I was unaware I'd said anything amusing, and I was at my most librarian-ish when I added, 'Really, Angel, we've got to stop standing around talking, and do something about this.'

'You're absolutely right,' Angel said. 'Let's put some tulip bulbs in potting soil on top of him. They'll come up great next year.'

'It's way too late to put in tulips,' I told her. Then, catching myself, feeling the day had already spun out of hand, I said, 'We've got to call the sheriff.'

'Oh, all right.' Angel stuck out her lip at me like a six-year-old whose fun had been spoiled, and laughed all the way into the house.

I hadn't seen Angel Youngblood laugh that much in the two years she'd been my bodyguard.

She was serious enough an hour later, when Padgett Lanier was sitting on my patio with a glass of iced coffee. Lanier was perhaps the most powerful man in our county. He'd been in office in one capacity or another for twenty years. If anyone knew where all the bodies were buried in Lawrenceton, Georgia, it was this man. With a heavy body, scanty blond hair, and invisible eyelashes, Lanier wasn't the most attractive man in my backyard, but he had a strong presence.

The 'most attractive man' prize had to go to my husband of two years, Martin Bartell, vice president of manufacturing at Pan-Am Agra, Lawrenceton's largest employer. Martin is a Vietnam vet, and at forty-seven he's fifteen years older than I. He pumps iron and plays various one-on-one competitive sports regularly, so his physique is impressive, and Martin has that devastating combination of white hair and black eyebrows. His eyes are light, light brown.

Angel's husband Shelby, who was lounging against the kitchen door, is swarthy and graying, with a Fu Manchu mustache and pockmarked cheeks. He is soft-spoken, polite, and an expert in the martial arts, as is Angel. Shelby and Martin are longtime friends.

Right now, Angel and I were the only women in sight. There were three deputies, the coroner, a local doctor, the sheriff, and our husbands. There were two men in the ambulance crew waiting to take 'the deceased' to – wherever they took things like that.

Lanier gave me a thorough head-to-toe evaluation, and I realized I was wearing shorts, a halter top, and dried sweat, and that my long and wayward hair was sloppily gathered into a band on top of my head. 'You musta been enjoying the sun, Miss Roe,' he said genially. 'A little early in the spring for it, ain't it?'

Now my friends call me Roe, but I'd never counted Lanier among them. I realized it was Lanier's way of handling a problem. I'd kept my own name when I'd married Martin, a decision on my part that I don't yet understand, since my laughable name had been the bane of my life. When you introduce yourself as 'Aurora Teagarden' you're going to get a snigger, if not a guffaw.

Padgett didn't know whether to call me Miss Teagarden, Mrs Teagarden, or Mrs Bartell, or Ms Teagarden-Bartell, and 'Miss Roe' was his compromise gesture.

My husband was watching the activity by the mower, standing with the relaxed attitude of a guy who comes home every day to find a man embedded in his lawn. That is to say, Martin was trying to look relaxed, but his gaze was following every move the lawmen made, and he was very busy thinking. I could tell because his mouth was an absolutely straight line, and his arms were crossed across his chest, the fingers twiddling: his Thinking Stance. The slightly taller Shelby lounged over to stand beside Martin, his hands stuck in his jeans pockets to show how relaxed *he* was. With the synchronicity born of long association, the two men turned and looked at each other, some silent comment about the fallen dead man passing between them.

I hadn't responded to Lanier, and he was waiting for me to say something.

'Well, we were taking turns mowing the lawn,' I answered. 'And that's always hot work. I did the front, so Angel took the back.' If I mow the front, I count it as my exercise for the day, and I don't have to pop in that stupid videotape and dance in front of the TV. We live a mile out of town, in the middle of fields, and we have a very large front yard, and a big back one.

Martin, listening, shook his head absently, as he always

did when my distaste for (most) strenuous physical activity crossed his mind. But he was still looking at the man embedded in our backyard.

'Do you think he'll be recognizable when he's turned over?' he asked the sheriff suddenly.

'No telling,' Lanier said. 'We've never had one dropped from a plane before. Now I wonder, do you suppose that body landed here on purpose?'

He had our full attention now, and he knew it. I felt a jolt of dismay.

'Would you like some more ice coffee?' I asked. (I know it's 'iced', but that's not what we say.)

He glanced at his glass. 'No, ma'am, I reckon I'm fine right now. Did that plane circle around before the man fell?'

I nodded. Lanier's gaze moved to Angel, where it dwelled wonderingly. She was something to see.

'Mrs Youngblood, you said you didn't see it?'

'No, Sheriff. I had the lawn mower running and I was listening to a tape.' Angel, who'd pulled a white T-shirt on over her bikini, was getting plenty of surreptitious attention from the deputies and the ambulance men. It ran off her like water off a duck's back. Angel is not pretty, but she is tall, very muscular and lean, and golden as a cheetah. Her legs are maybe a mile long.

'Miss Roe, you actually saw him fall?'

'Yes. But I didn't see him come out of the plane. When I looked up, he was already in the air.'

'You reckon he was already dead?'

I hadn't considered that. 'Yes,' I said slowly. 'Yes, I think he was. Because he was . . .' I had to take a deep breath. 'He was all floppy.'

Martin moved behind me and put his hands on my shoulders.

Padgett Lanier shook his glass a little to hear the ice cubes tinkle against the sides. 'I wonder, when we turn the deceased over, if you all would mind taking a look at him.' He held up a placatory hand before we could respond. 'I know, I know, it's an awful thing to ask anyone, especially these ladies, but we do need to know if you have seen this man anytime or anywhere, before today.'

I had never wanted to do anything less. My husband's hands gripped my shoulders bracingly.

'Sheriff! We're ready when you are!' called the taller of the deputies, as he pulled on an extra pair of plastic gloves. Lanier heaved himself out of his chair and strode over to the body.

This was a process I did not want to watch, and I covered my face with my hands. I heard some sounds I definitely didn't want to match to an image.

'You needn't bother, ladies,' called Lanier. His voice was very unsteady. I wondered if I ought to tell him where the bathroom was. 'You needn't bother,' he said again, in a lower voice. But the people in our yard were so quiet, it was easy to hear. 'I recognize him myself . . . I think.'

I dropped my hands in amazement, caught a glimpse of what was being lifted from the lawn, and put them back up hurriedly.

'Who is it?' Martin called, close to my ear.

'Detective Sergeant Jack Burns, City of Lawrenceton Police Department.'

Padgett Lanier, no doubt about it, had a certain sense of ceremony.

After some dreadful minutes, the envelope of broken bones and jellied organs that was Jack Burns's body was maneuvered into a bag and then into the ambulance. Lanier, obviously shaken but still maintaining his official face, ambled over to the patio. I was feeling very shaky, and Angel was an interesting shade of green. I thought she might be sick again. Martin and Shelby looked even grimmer than they had before.

'How long has it been since you saw Jack Burns?' Lanier asked me. 'Seems to me as though you and he never got along too well, am I right?'

'I never had any quarrel with Mr Burns,' I said steadily. That was the truth. Jack Burns's dislike of me had not had its basis in any one incident, but in cumulative distrust. 'And I haven't seen him in – maybe years.' Which had been fine with me; I'd feared Jack, with his blind zeal for his own brand of justice. It's bad to have a policeman as an enemy.

'And you, Mrs Youngblood?'

'We did have a run-in a couple of weeks ago,' Angel said calmly, though her color betrayed her. I tried not to show any surprise.

'And just what was that about—?'

'He ticketed my car downtown, for some completely bullshit city ordinance he'd looked up in the books.'

'Now why would he do that?'

Angel put her hands on her hips, and her arm muscles rippled. 'I came out of the bank and found him putting a ticket on my car and we had a little talk, kind of sharp.'

'Anyone around during this little talk?'

'Sure,' Angel said wearily. 'It was downtown on a Friday

morning. I saw that man that works at the library with Roe – Perry Allison – and I saw that pretty round woman who works at Marcus Hatfield, the one with the dark hair who has the little girl.'

'Carey Osland,' Lanier decided.

'Right, if you say so.' Angel seemed indifferent to the question of the woman's name.

Martin looked at me, his eyebrows arched: Did you know about this? I shook my head almost imperceptibly.

'Why do you think, Mrs Youngblood, that a detective sergeant would give a parking ticket?'

'Because he thought it was Roe's car,' Angel said bluntly. 'We both have blue Chevettes. Mine's the same age, I got it used. Though mine's a slightly different shade of blue, we basically have the same car.'

'Did you have a conversation with Jack Burns?'

'Not what you would call a conversation,' Angel said dryly. 'He looked kind of taken aback when he saw it was my car, but then it was like he figured if I lived out here in Roe's garage apartment, giving me a ticket was almost as good as giving her one. And he was right, I probably *was* seven inches from the curb instead of six. But I wasn't in a good mood.'

This had been a real speech for Angel, who did not tend to be chatty. But Padgett Lanier wanted more.

'So you had words?' he prodded her.

Angel sighed. 'I asked him why he was giving me a ticket and he told me I was parked too far from the curb, and he asked me how Roe was doing, had she found any more bodies lately, and I told him he was giving me a bullshit ticket, and he said he was sure there was some ordinance still on the books about public bad language, and did I want to see if I could karate-chop my way out of a jail cell.'

Lanier stared at her, fascinated. 'And what did you say?'

'Nothing.'

'You didn't respond?'

'No point to it. He'd decided he was going to give me the ticket.'

Lanier seemed nonplused. He eyed Angel a moment or two longer, then asked Martin if he'd seen Jack Burns lately.

'The last time I saw Jack Burns was two years ago, about the time I met my wife,' Martin said calmly. His fingers dug into the tight muscles of my neck and I tilted my head back.

'And you, Mr Youngblood?'

'Hadn't ever met him.'

'You weren't mad about your wife getting a ticket?'

'If you park seven inches from the curb, you gotta take what's coming to you.'

Padgett Lanier's pale face had a tendency to flush easily. We watched now with some trepidation as he turned a tomato red. The sheriff dismissed us curtly, and turned his attention to the search his men were making in our yard. I wanted to beg them not to trample my poor little just-plowed garden, but I decided that would be unfeeling.

With the passage of a couple of hours, supper had become just possible. I called the Youngbloods' apartment to ask Shelby and Angel if they wanted to share our meal, but Angel said she'd rather lie down than eat, and Shelby didn't want to leave her.

Martin and I had pork chops, fried green tomatoes (a rare indulgence), Waldorf salad, and I'd made some biscuits. But we were just picking at the food. Martin had been quiet throughout the meal, which was unusual. Normally, we talked to each other at the table, before we went about our separate pursuits in the evening. (Sometimes they were mutual pursuits, but that usually came later. About bedtime.)

Our house felt very quiet after the onslaught of county and city police. We hadn't had that many people around since the last year's Christmas party.

'Roe, I'm worried about this,' Martin said finally. His pale brown eyes focused on me; Martin looks into the eyes of the people he's talking to. That can be intimidating, or exciting.

'I know. I am, too, of course.'

'Not just Jack Burns being killed, but him being dumped here.'

'Of course,' I said again, not understanding what Martin was getting at.

'As Sheriff Lanier pointed out, people know that you and he didn't get along.'

'But I was absolutely, provably on the ground when he landed. So I couldn't have done it,' I said dismissively. 'Besides which, I can't fly a plane.'

'There's something wrong about it.' Martin was having some problem formulating his thoughts, unusual for him. He's used to expressing himself quickly and decisively in front of a lot of people.

I didn't want to say 'Of course,' again, but that was what I was thinking.

'How long has it been since you talked to him?' Martin asked.

'The sheriff asked me that this afternoon. The best I can recall, I haven't seen Jack to speak to since . . . two and a half years ago at the Anderton house. Same as you.' The day Martin and I had met. He smiled at me now, warmly but briefly, to show me he, too, remembered that day very well.

'Did you think Angel reacted normally today?' Martin said suddenly.

'No, I don't think so at all,' I said, glad he'd said it instead of me. 'I don't know what's wrong with her. Angel's not one to flinch away from anything unpleasant, and she has the strongest stomach of anyone I know. For some reason, this just threw her for a loop.' And I remembered Jack Burns rotating in the air, and was sorry I'd used that expression. I put my napkin by my plate and pushed the plate away.

'Something's up with her,' Martin said. 'I could tell Shelby was worried, too. And I could swear he'd never heard this story about the ticket.'

'Would you mind doing the dishes tonight?'

'No.' Martin seemed glad to shake off whatever dark thoughts he'd been having. 'Are you going out? Is it Friends of the Library night, or some church meeting?'

'No,' I said. 'I've got to go pay my condolences to Bess Burns.'

'Roe, do you think that's wise?'

'I've always liked her, even if I didn't like him. I've gotten to know her at Friends meetings.'

Since I'd resumed working at the library on a part-time basis, I'd met everyone who worked there as a volunteer. And Bess Burns, since she'd retired from teaching, was one of our best workers.

Martin continued to look at me in a troubled way, but he nodded. 'I don't mind doing the dishes,' he said. 'Have you fed that cat yet?'

'I'll do it before I go,' I promised. Martin and Madeleine, the fat old cat I inherited from a friend, have a touchy relationship at best. Madeleine's favorite perch is the hood of Martin's Mercedes-Benz, and Martin is very proud of that car. We even got doors installed on the garage and we check to be sure they're closed every night, but we have to search for Madeleine before we do.

I went up the stairs in a hurry, mentally selecting my visit-to-the-widow outfit. Not black, I wasn't a member of the family . . . navy. My new navy blue dress with the white trim. I'd just bought it at Short 'N Sweet in Atlanta – a petite shop, I'm four eleven – and I glanced at the label, gloating over the smaller size I'd been buying lately, before I pulled it over my head.

Living with a health- and exercise-conscious man like Martin, and having the athletic Angel as a companion, had had a happy result as far as my figure was concerned. I'd even gone to the beauty shop my mother patronizes, Clip Casa, and gotten Benita to streak my hair. It took hours, since it's thick, tightly wavy, and halfway down my back. But the result was worth it. Overall, what with being happy with Martin and secure financially, I looked and felt better than I had at any time in my life.

After wiggling into pantyhose – a process I wouldn't let Martin watch – I slid my feet into pumps and pulled my frivolous streaky hair back with a barrette. I fed Madeleine hastily, grabbed my food offering from the refrigerator, and backed out my old Chevette, a car Martin detests almost as much as he detests Madeleine's paw prints.

Though we live a mile out of town, I can almost see the back of my mother's house from my own backyard, and the Burns home was only one street south of hers. But it was a street that made a lot of difference; Mother's home on Plantation was a roomy two-storey with a large lot, and Bess and Jack owned a fairly modest three-bedroom ranch.

There were two cars parked in front of the Burns home, one of them a familiar blue Lincoln Continental. It would have taken Mother five minutes to walk, but she would never willingly arrive anywhere flushed with exertion. Mother was actually coming toward me with a bowl in her hand as I got out of my old car, clutching my own dish.

'What you got there?' I asked.

'A cold pasta salad. It's all I had in the house to make.'

My mother, Aida Brattle Teagarden Queensland, is a slim, husky-voiced Lauren Bacall look-alike. She is also a very successful Realtor, and a few short years ago she married John Queensland, a retired businessman. Since then, she's become a stepgrandmother a couple of times. Once the shock wore off, she's enjoyed it.

I peered through the plastic wrap. 'Looks good.'

'Thanks. I see you brought your Waldorf salad. Well, are you going to ring the doorbell?'

I did so, and the door swung open after the correct interval. The Burns's neighbor to the right, Marva Clerrick, had on her formal smile. It changed into a less strained one when she recognized us.

'Am I glad to see you!' she exclaimed in a violent

whisper. 'The strangest people are here talking to Bess! I have no idea what's going on!'

Marva, an athletic extrovert and the wife of my sometime boss, Sam Clerrick, was one of the most popular teachers at Lawrenceton High School and a good friend of the recently retired Bess Burns. Marva had been aptly named by parents who must have had some premonition that Marva would be able to cook, teach English during the week and Sunday School at Western Hill Baptist Church, bring up two very good girls, and cope with the moody Sam. In the summer, her off-season, Marva taught swimming at the local pool and led rug-hooking classes at Peachtree Leisure Apartments.

For Marva to be confounded by a situation, it must be strange indeed. Of course, we were agog.

'What's going on?' I asked in a stage whisper.

'There are two men here I've never seen before in this town,' Marva hissed back. 'And to fall out of a plane! How could that happen by accident? What was Jack doing up in a plane?'

'I hate to bring this up, but I think Jack was already dead when he came out of the plane,' I said hesitantly. No one had asked me not to tell, and if Mother found out from another source she'd never forgive me.

'Already dead?' my mother said. She and Marva stared at me with twin expressions of distaste, fascination, and horror.

'He sure looked like it,' I said, involuntarily seeing the body turning in the air. 'Of course, someone else was flying the plane.'

'Oh, girl, you don't mean you *saw* it?' Marva asked breathlessly.

I nodded, surprised at this failure of the rumor mill.

'I heard it was that young woman that lives in your apartment out there, the gal with all the muscles,' Marva said indignantly.

'Oh, we were both out in the backyard.'

'Did you see the airplane, too?' Mother asked.

I shrugged. 'It was just a little ole plane, red and white. I didn't notice any of the numbers on it.' It would be hard to find someone who knew less about airplanes than I did.

'I can't believe it, in our little town,' Marva said, forgetting to whisper. 'Maybe it was somebody Jack had sent to prison?'

Mother and I shrugged simultaneously, and shook our heads to back the shrug up.

'Well, see what you make of this situation here, and let me know,' Marva said. 'I've been minding the door for an hour now, but I have to go home soon, I've got bread coming out of the oven and I don't know if Sissy will remember to get it out of the loaf pan after ten minutes' sitting.'

'Where is Bess?' my mother asked directly, tired of all this hissing by the front door.

'Straight through,' Marva said, nodding her head at the door at the rear of the foyer. 'The kids haven't gotten here yet, but she's talked to both of them on the phone. They have long drives.' I remembered the Burns children, Jack Junior and Romney, went to different colleges in different states.

'We'll put our bowls in the refrigerator before we talk to her,' Mother told Marva firmly.

Bess's kitchen looked just like mine usually did, basically clean but messy around the edges, with bills sticking out of a letter caddy on the wall and an open box of teabags by a pitcher. Another neighbor was working out her helpful impulses by wiping the counter, and we smiled and nodded at each other in a subdued way.

I opened the refrigerator to put in my offering. It was half-full of similar dishes, plastic-wrapped food that people had brought to Bess Burns in her time of trouble, to help feed her surely incoming family. By noon tomorrow, there would be no available shelf space.

Somehow reassured by the correctness of the refrigerator, Mother and I made our way to the den at the back of the house.

Bess was sitting on the couch with two big men flanking her. I'd never seen either man before. They wore suits, and ties, and grim expressions, and as the slim red-haired widow blotted her face with a white handkerchief, they offered her no comfort.

'We're so sorry,' Mother said, in a perfectly calibrated tone of sympathy calculated not to start the tears again.

'Thank you,' Bess said. Bess's voice was almost expressionless from exhaustion and shock. The lines across her forehead and from nose to mouth looked deeper, and traces of red lipstick stood out garishly on her pale face. 'I appreciate you coming, and Aurora, too,' Bess said with great effort.

I bent awkwardly across the coffee table to give her a hug. Bess, who had only retired at the end of the previous school year, was still wearing her schoolteacher clothes, one of those relaxed cotton knit pants sets with the loose tunic. Hers was blue with a giant red apple on the front. It seemed ludicrously cheerful.

'Do they know why, yet—?' my mother said, as if she had a perfect right to ask.

Bess actually, opened her mouth to answer, when the blond man to her right held up a hand to silence her. He stared up at us from behind tortoise-shell-framed glasses.

'It's still under investigation,' he said heavily.

Mother and I glanced at each other.

Mother was not to be bested on her own territory. 'I am Aida Queensland, a neighbor,' she said pointedly. 'I don't believe I've met you?'

'I'm John Dryden from Atlanta,' he said, which was an answer that told us nothing.

I didn't like people being rude to my mother.

'You would be Mr Pope, then,' I said to the other man, who was darker and younger.

'Pope?' He stared at me curiously. 'No. I'm Don O'Riley. From Atlanta.'

Though Mother was trying to give me a censorious face, she was really stifling a smile.

'Bess, why don't you come with us out to the kitchen?' I said. 'Show us what we should put out for you and your friends to eat.' They clearly weren't friends, and whoever they were, they were upsetting Bess even more than she already was. 'It's so late, and I'm sure you haven't had a thing.'

'No, I haven't eaten,' she said, looking as though she liked being talked to directly. Before her two 'friends' could stop her, she stood up and circled the coffee table to go to the kitchen with us.

The neighbor who'd been there had left, leaving behind spotless counters and a feeling of goodwill. Bess stood and stared as though she didn't recognize her own appliances.

'Were they bothering you?' Mother asked.

'They have to, it's their job,' Bess said, with the weary endurance of a law enforcement wife. 'I shouldn't say anything about this, but Jack knew the identity of a – person – here in town who's been hidden . . . well, I better not say any more. They wonder if it might be related to his being killed.'

'Ah,' said Mother with great significance, which was more than I could think of to say. She turned to fiddle with a dish of spaghetti she'd gotten from the refrigerator, and I saw her eyes close as if she was wondering how in the hell she'd gotten into this kitchen hearing this fascinating but bizarre revelation.

'You saw him fall, Roe,' Bess said directly to me. The air of exhaustion was gone, and in its place was a dreadful intensity. 'Was he dead when he fell, or did he die from the impact?'

'I think he was dead when he came out of the plane,' I said, trying not to cry in the face of her pain, since she was keeping her own tears in check. 'I don't think he felt a thing, or ever knew he was falling.'

'Thank you,' she said quietly.

'Mrs Burns, here you are,' said the blond Mr Dryden sharply, though he could have had little doubt about Bess's location. He was tucking his glasses into his breast pocket. Without them, his face looked even more alert. 'You have a phone call you need to take in the living room. Ladies, thanks for coming to see Mrs Burns in her time of grief.'

None of us had heard the phone ring.

'We'll just set your meal out, and then we'll leave,' Mother said firmly. 'Bess, if you need us, we'll be *right here*.'

'Thanks so much,' John Dryden said – dryly. And damned if he didn't stay in the kitchen, watching us get out paper plates (since we couldn't feature Dryden and O'Riley helping with the dishes) and heat up spaghetti in the built-in microwave. We prepared three plates of spaghetti, Waldorf salad, and green bean casserole, and set the table as best we could, what with having to search for the forks and napkins and glasses.

'Mr Dryden,' said my mother, as he escorted us to the front door without our having caught another glimpse of Bess, 'can you tell us when the funeral will be, and the name of the funeral home? I need to arrange for some flowers.'

'I don't believe we're certain at this time about any of that,' Dryden said cautiously. 'There has to be an autopsy.'

So Dryden was a stranger to Bess Burns, if not to Jack. Any Lawrenceton native would know the Burns's burials would be from Jasper Funeral Home, since Jerry Saylor of Saylor's Funeral Home had divorced Bess Burns's sister. From the way Mother and I looked at each other, Dryden knew he'd said something significant; you could see him trying to figure it out, abandoning the attempt.

'I suppose the funeral date will be in the obituary in tomorrow's paper?' my mother persisted.

He looked blank.

'I'm sure it will be,' he said.

We didn't believe him for a minute.

'Jack Junior and Romney had better get home quick,' my mother said darkly as she slid her elegant legs into her car.

I drove home slowly, more questions in my mind than I'd had when I'd set out.

Chapter Two

'I think Dryden and Pope – I mean, O'Riley – were some kind of federal agents,' I told Martin as he pulled on his maroon pajama bottoms that night. He just uses the bottoms, except on very cold nights, and we don't get too many of those in Lawrenceton. I've never figured out what to do with the tops. Sometimes *I* wear them. 'FBI or CIA or federal marshals.'

'As long as they weren't interested in me,' Martin said.

'You're out of all that now. Jack's death couldn't have anything to do with you, no matter who's investigating it.'

Discovering Martin's secret life had been the most terrible blow I'd ever sustained. Martin was born to be a buccaneer. For a while his love of danger had been satisfied by a brief stint working for a shadowy CIA-funded company following the war. After he'd begun working for Pan-Am Agra, he'd been approached again, and had resumed his clandestine activities. Only his complete withdrawal from the gun smuggling he'd been facilitating on his legitimate business trips to Central America had made our marriage workable.

I had just about recovered from the fact that he hadn't told me anything about it before we married; but it had taken a while. For a couple of months, separation had been a real possibility.

I didn't like remembering that time. Angel and Shelby dated from those days also, but I'd managed to regard them as friends and employees rather than bodyguards, for the most part. Martin had made some enemies along the way in his clandestine trade, and he was out of town a lot; installing Shelby and Angel had seemed like a wise precaution to him. Though Shelby had at first worked at Pan-Am Agra as cover for his real job – guarding me – it looked as if he actually had a career there now. He'd risen to crew leader and another promotion was looming on the horizon. That seemed the oddest by-product of the whole thing.

As I was sitting in our king-size bed with my crossword puzzle book on a lap desk resting on my knees, the thought occurred to me that, like Martin, Jack Burns was a tough man with a few enemies.

Jack, who must have been in his early fifties, had spent most of his working career on the Lawrenceton police force, though I remembered he'd tried the Atlanta police for a four-year stint. Jack had hated Atlanta ever after, and more than just about any other resident of Lawrenceton, he had resented our town's ever-nearing inclusion in the sprawling Atlanta metroplex. Jack had hated change, and loved justice, which couldn't come pure enough to suit him. He'd had an almost total disregard for his personal appearance, beyond getting his hair cut and shaving every morning; he'd always looked as though he'd reached in his closet blindfolded and pulled on whatever came out, pieces that often seemed totally unrelated to each other.

'I wonder how he came to be in the plane,' I murmured, putting aside the lap desk and book. 'Seems like to me he took flying lessons at one time. I think I remember Bess saying he thought it might come in handy on the job.'

Martin was brushing his teeth, but he heard me. He appeared in the bathroom door to make gestures. He'd tell me in a minute.

I heard gargling noises, and Martin emerged blotting his mouth with a towel, which he tossed back in the bathroom as an afterthought. It landed sort of in the vicinity of the towel rack.

He's not good about hanging up towels.

'While you were out tonight,' he said, 'Sally called.'

I raised my eyebrows interrogatively. Sally Allison was the kingpin reporter for the *Lawrenceton Sentinel*.

'She wanted you to know, for some reason, that Jack Burns had rented the plane himself, from the Starry Night Airport ten miles away on the interstate.'

'He rented it *himself*?'

Martin nodded.

Good friend that Sally was, she knew I'd be intrigued by that little fact. I clipped my pencil to the puzzle book and tried to imagine how someone had gotten Jack into the plane and then killed him and thrown him out; could one person do that? Could little planes be set on autopilot? Wouldn't someone be at the airfield to monitor arrivals and departures?

'From the very little Burns's wife said to you, he knew the identity of someone here in Lawrenceton who'd been hidden by the Federal Witness Protection Program,' Martin said.

'So why would the – I don't know, what do you call 'em, protectee? Why would he kill Jack?'

Martin raised his eyebrows at me. I'd missed something very obvious.

'I imagine whoever killed Jack Burns wanted the new name of the hidden person.'

Naturally. I should have seen that before. 'But if these were the people this witness had testified against, wouldn't they know what he looked like?'

'Maybe he's had plastic surgery,' Martin said. 'Or maybe these people only suspect they know who betrayed them.' But his interest in the subject had ebbed. Once he'd decided we were safe, not implicated, he'd begun losing interest in Jack Burns's death, except as it upset or concerned me.

'But why in our backyard, Martin? You were worried about that earlier,' I challenged him. 'Let's hear a good reason.' I took off my glasses (I was wearing my blue-framed ones that day) and crossed my arms under my breasts. They were more or less covered in ivory lace, the top of a concoction Martin had given me for his birthday.

'Do you think our yard was picked on purpose?' Martin asked.

'Yes . . . maybe. I didn't want to make a song and dance about it when Padgett Lanier was here, but the plane circled to get the drop right. The body could have been dumped in any of the fields around here and lain for days with no one the wiser and no way to trace the plane. They risked Angel and me seeing the plane, to dump Jack *here*.' I pointed down, as if our bed had been the target.

'It was a threat against the protectee, as you call him,' Martin said calmly. He seemed to feel better about the implications of Jack Burns ending up in our yard now.

'Saying, "Here is the body of the man who knew you, we're coming to get you soon".'

'Could be. But why here?'

'They wanted the body found as soon as possible, to get their message across. They saw a nice big yard with two women in it who were sure to call the police right away.'

Not for the first time, I realized how much I'd come to rely on Martin's decisiveness and authority. If he said this was nothing for me to worry about, I was fairly willing to accept it. And I also recognized something I should have spotted earlier; my husband was furious. Protective Martin did not like his wife frightened by falling bodies, especially when he'd decided the body had fallen near her by design. Martin was as full of pressure as a preemptive volcano.

It was too bad we didn't have a home racquetball court. That was Martin's favorite method of letting off steam.

He had another one, however.

'Martin, I was really scared today.'

Instantly he moved to his side of the bed and slid in, and his arms went around me. I nestled my head in the hollow of his neck. He held me carefully, delicately. I know a man's protection is illusory, but illusions can be awfully comforting sometimes. I raised my face to his and kissed him. When I was sure we were both thinking the same thing, I switched off my bedside lamp, turned back to him, and gave his neck a tiny nip.

We were much more relaxed when we went to sleep.

Sally Allison's story in the *Lawrenceton Sentinel* the next day said nothing about two big men from Atlanta. Martin left it folded open on the table by a clean coffee cup, waiting for me; he'd had to go in early for a breakfast meeting with his division heads.

Jack Burns, longtime member of the Lawrenceton police force, was killed sometime early Monday afternoon. His body, thrown from a low-flying airplane, landed on the property of Aurora Teagarden and Martin Bartell, about a mile out of town on Mason Road, at approximately 2 P.M. yesterday.

Burns, a native of Lawrenceton, was not known to have any enemies. His wife, former teacher Bess Linton Burns, expressed bafflement at the motive for her husband's death. 'I can only think it must have been someone he arrested, someone out for revenge,' she said.

'The means of his death are not known now,' stated Sheriff Padgett Lanier. 'Only the autopsy can tell us that.'

Lanier went on to say the sheriff's department is investigating how someone else could have entered the Piper plane, rented by Burns from Starry Night Airport yesterday, and overcome Burns. The plane was found returned yesterday, and no one at the tiny airport can identify the pilot.

See Obituaries, Page 6.

I could imagine Sally's frustration at being given so little to work with. When she'd called me the night before to offer me the tidbit about Jack Burns himself having rented the plane that took him to his final landing place, perhaps she'd been in search of some additional detail to pad out the story. Accompanying it was the usual grim shot of the two medics loading the covered stretcher into the ambulance.

You could tell the covered bundle was sort of flat – I gulped and pushed the memory away.

I glanced at the clock. It was a relief to have to look at it again, to have something to plan my days around. I'd resumed working part-time at the library in Lawrenceton four weeks ago when Sam Clerrick had called me out of the blue to tell me his oldest librarian had suddenly turned to him to say, 'I can't shelve one more book. I can't tell one more child to be quiet. I can't deal with this new aide. I can't tell one more patron where the Georgia collection is.'

Left in a bind, Sam had called me since I'd worked for him before. I'd agreed instantly to take the job; and Sam had agreed to see how my working part-time would do, at least while he scouted around to see if anyone wanted to work full-time. So I was working nine to one for five days a week, with one of the days changing every week, since the library was open on Saturdays from nine to one. No one wanted Saturday every week, including me. The aide took over in the afternoons, sometimes in conjunction with a volunteer.

I was ready to go in early. Might as well get the inevitable inquisition from my co-workers over with.

It was a beautiful spring Tuesday, with lots of sun and a brisk cool breeze. Angel was sitting on the steps leading up to the Youngbloods' garage apartment, looking muddy, the result of pallor under her chronic tan.

'What's the matter?' I couldn't remember Angel ever being ill.

'I don't know,' she said. 'The past few days I've just felt awful. I don't want to get up out of bed, I don't want to run.'

'Do you have a temperature?'

'No,' she said listlessly. 'At least, I don't think so. We've never had a thermometer.'

I tried to imagine that. 'Did you try to run today?'

'Yeah. I got about half a mile and had to come back.' She was still in her running clothes, sweating profusely.

'Look, let me take you in to the doctor. I've got an hour before I really have to be at work,' I said impulsively. I hated to think of Angel driving to the doctor by herself; she was so obviously ill.

'I've never been to a doctor except to get stitched up in an emergency room,' Angel said.

'Let me go call him,' I said, when I'd recovered from my shock. 'You go take a shower and pull on some slacks.'

Angel nodded wearily and pulled herself up by the railing. She was trudging the stairs as I went inside to call the doctor and the library. 'I promise I'll work the hours today,' I told Sam. 'I just have to take a friend to the doctor. She hasn't got anyone else.'

'There are disadvantages to having an employee who doesn't really need the job,' Sam said distantly. 'Is this going to be happening much?'

'No,' I said, a little offended, though I knew he was in the right. 'I'll be in on time tomorrow. It's just today that I'll be a little late.'

When I got out to my old blue car, Angel was sitting on the passenger's side in white slacks and a yellow tank top, though it seemed cool for a tank top to me. I remembered how profusely she'd been sweating after her short run. She was leaning her head against the glass of the window.

Angel's indisposition was worrying me more and more. I'd never seen her anything less than 100 percent physically, and I'd always envied her Superwoman physique – though not enough to work out every day so I'd have one like it. Angel was silent and listless during the short ride into town.

Dr Zelman's waiting room was not as full as I'd feared. There were two elderly couples; probably only one out of each pair needed to see the doctor. And oddly enough, there was blond Mr Dryden, who was arguing with Dr Zelman's receptionist, Trinity.

'Would you please inform the doctor that I'm here on official business?' Dryden was saying in an exasperated voice.

'I did,' Trinity said coldly.

I could have given Mr Dryden some good advice right about then, had he been in the market for it. 'Never alienate the receptionist' is the first rule of all those who have a limited pool of doctors to draw from.

'Does he realize that I need to get back to Atlanta very soon?'

'He does indeed realize that.' Trinity's face under its fluff of brown-and-gray permed hair was getting grimmer and grimmer.

'You're sure you told him?'

'I tell Dr Zelman everything. I'm his wife.'

Dryden resumed his seat in a chastened manner. It seemed the only two adjacent seats in the waiting room were the ones next to him. After we'd filled out the necessary 'new patient' and insurance forms, Angel and I settled in, with me next to Dryden. I wriggled in my seat, resigned to discomfort. My feet can never quite touch the floor in standard chairs. So I often have to sit with my knees primly together, toes braced on the floor. I was wearing khakis that morning, and a sky-blue blouse with a button-down collar. My hair, loose today since I'd been in a hurry to get Angel to the doctor, kept getting wrapped around the buttons. Since Angel obviously didn't feel like talking, once I'd disentangled myself I opened a paperback (I always keep one in my purse) and was soon deep in the happenings of Jesus Creek, Tennessee.

'Aren't your glasses a different color today?' inquired a male voice.

I glanced up. Dryden was staring at me. 'I have several pairs,' I told him. I had on my white-rimmed ones today, to celebrate spring.

His blond brows rose slightly above his heavy tortoiseshell rims. 'Expensive,' he said. 'You must have married an optometrist.'

'No,' I said. 'I'm rich.'

That kept him quiet for a while, but not long enough.

'Are you the same Aurora Teagarden into whose yard the body fell yesterday?' he asked, when the silence seemed to stretch.

No, I'm a different one. There are several of us in Lawrenceton. 'Yes.'

'And you didn't say anything at the Burns house last night?'

'What was I supposed to say?' I asked, bewildered. ' "Gee, Mrs Burns, I saw your husband's body. It looked as though someone had run over it with a meat tenderizer"? Actually, she did ask me if he was dead before he hit the ground and I told her I thought he was.'

'I see.'

About damn time.

31

'However,' he continued, 'we need to interview you about the incident.'

I noted the terminology. 'Then you'll have to do it this afternoon. I have to go to work after I take my friend home. And I have to get my husband off to Chicago.' I added this last out of sheer perversity, since Martin, experienced traveler that he was, always packed for himself and drove himself to the airport in a company car, not wanting his Mercedes to be the target of thieves or vandals in the long-term parking lot. The only thing I had to do with Martin's trips was to miss him.

I'd been missing him a lot lately.

Dryden suggested four o'clock at my house, I agreed, and I returned pointedly to my book. But Dryden had his talking shoes on.

'So, your husband is the plant manager at Pan-Am Agra?'

'His job just got upgraded to vice president in charge of manufacturing.' I turned a page.

'Have you been married long?'

By golly, I was on the verge of being rude. Really.

'Two years,' I said briefly.

Then, thank goodness, Trinity called Angel's name.

'Please come in with me, Roe,' my bodyguard said quietly.

Considerably surprised, but pleased to be escaping Dryden, I tucked my book in my purse and rose to my feet. Dr Zelman's new nurse took over from Trinity, leading us to a cramped examining room with rose-and-blue walls and a table that would barely hold Angel. Something about the nurse seemed familiar. As she talked to Angel about her aches and pains, efficiently taking Angel's blood pressure and checking her temperature, I realized the woman in white was Linda Ehrhardt, whose bridesmaid I'd been in the long, long ago. She'd been Linda Pocock for years now. As she turned away from Angel, she recognized me too.

After the usual exclamations and hugs, Linda said, 'I guess you heard I got divorced and moved back home.'

'I'm sorry. But it'll be nice to see you again.'

'Yes, that'll be fun. Of course I brought my children, and they're in school here now.'

'I'm sorry, I've forgotten. Was that two girls?'

'Yes, Carol and Macey.' Linda extracted the thermometer from Angel's mouth and glanced at the reading. She wrote it down on Angel's chart without a change of expression.

'Mrs Youngblood, you'll need to disrobe for your examination,' Linda said rather loudly, as though Angel's habitual silence meant she was short on wits rather than words. 'There's the cubicle in the corner, just put on one of those gowns.'

Angel glared at Linda after she'd looked at the cubicle, and I had to admit I couldn't see Angel's changing in that tiny area as a possibility. But she managed, grumbling to herself. So I wouldn't be just sitting there listening to her, I brushed my hair with the help of the mirror over the sink, carefully drawing the brush all the way through the mass of streaky brown waves, trying not to break off my ends by pulling the brush out too soon. I gave up when it was flying around my head, wild with electricity. By that time Angel had managed to reensconce herself on the table with the obligatory sheet across her lap, though she was clearly unhappy with the whole situation and not a little afraid.

Dr Zelman burst in just as Angel was about to say

something. He never just came into a room, and he never just left; he made entrances and exits. He almost never closed the door completely, something his nurse or his patient's friends had to do. (I crept behind him to do it now.) Now in his early fifties, 'Pinky' (Pincus) Zelman had worked in Lawrenceton for twenty years, after a short-lived practice in Augusta that had left him inexplicably longing for something more rural.

'Mrs Youngblood!' he cried happily. 'You're so healthy you've never been to see me before, in two years here, I see! Good for you! What can I do for you today?' Dr Zelman caught sight of me trying to be unobtrusively solicitous, and patted me on the shoulder so heavily I almost went down. 'Little Ms Teagarden! Prettier than ever!' I smiled uneasily as he turned back to Angel.

Angel stoically recited her symptoms: occasional exhaustion, occasional queasiness, lack of energy. I winced when I thought of asking Angel to help me mow the yard the day before. Now quiet and intent, Dr Zelman began examining her from head to toe, including a pelvic, which Angel clearly hadn't expected (I hadn't either) and which she barely endured.

'Well, Mrs Youngblood,' Dr Zelman said thoughtfully, rooting for his pencil in his graying hair (it was stuck behind his ear), 'it's really too bad your husband didn't come with you today, because we have a lot to talk about.'

Angel and I both blanched. I reached out and grabbed her hand.

'Because, of course, Mrs Youngblood, as I'm sure you guessed, you *are* pregnant.'

Angel and I gasped simultaneously.

'I'm sure you knew, right? You must have missed two periods. You're at least ten weeks along, maybe more. Of course, with your wonderful physique, you're not showing.'

'I'm not regular at all,' Angel said in a stunned way. 'I really didn't notice, and it didn't occur to me to wonder, because my husband . . . has had a vasectomy.'

I sat down abruptly. Fortunately, there was a chair underneath.

For once, Dr Zelman looked nonplused. 'Has he had a recheck done recently?' he asked.

'Recheck? He got snipped! Why should he have a recheck?' For once, Angel's voice rose.

'It's wise, Mrs Youngblood, wise indeed, to have that recheck. Sometimes the severed tubes grow back. I'm sorry I gave you the news so blithely, since it seems you and your husband had not planned to have any children. But a baby's on the way, Mrs Youngblood. Well on the way. You're in such excellent condition and so slim that the baby may not show at all for another month or so, especially since this must be your first pregnancy.'

Angel was shaking her head from side to side, disbelievingly.

'If your husband wants to talk to me,' Dr Zelman said gently, 'I can explain to him how this happened.'

'I'm pretty sure he's going to think he knows already,' Angel said dismally. 'But I would never in this world . . .' She shook her head, finishing the rest of her sentence in her head.

★

I had to help Angel dress, she was so deeply shocked. I tried not to burble, since she was upset, but I was so excited by proxy that it was hard.

A baby.

'How can I work?' Angel said, but not as if she was really concerned.

'Pooh, as a bodyguard? I don't need a bodyguard any-more, now that Martin's out of – that mess,' I said sooth-ingly. 'If you still want to help me out around the place, we'll work something out. Maybe I could keep the baby for you? Some?'

She heard the yearning in my voice.

'This should be happening to you,' she said with a faint smile on her thin lips.

'Oh, Martin's worried about his age,' I said, and thought right away of kicking myself: Shelby Youngblood was Martin's age, forty-seven, and Angel was twenty-eight to my thirty-two and a half. 'Anyway,' I said bracingly, 'you tell him to call Dr Zelman, okay? He may get kind of upset, having had a vasectomy and all.'

'Oh, I just bet he will,' she said grimly.

Angel walked out to the car in a state of stunned silence. I made sure she was in the car and then I ran back in to get my purse, which I'd left in the examining room. You could tell I was excited and upset, since normally I'd be as likely to leave my arm as my purse. I explained to Trinity Zelman, who waved me on back, and Linda was waiting at the door to the examining room with the purse in hand.

'Knew you'd come back for it,' she said. 'Give me a call, now!' She hurried down the hall to the little lab, and I turned to go out, passing the first examining room on one side and Dr Zelman's office on the other on my way to the waiting room. Dr Zelman's office door was typically ajar, and I heard Mr Dryden's pleasant accentless voice inside. He'd finally gotten his five minutes with the doctor.

'I see that the widow has urged me to talk with you about her husband's condition,' Dr Zelman was saying without much enthusiasm. 'So I'll answer your questions.'

I walked slower.

'In your opinion, was Jack Burns an alcoholic?' Dryden asked directly.

'Yes,' said Dr Zelman. 'Just this past two or three years, he came to me on several occasions with drink-related injuries. He'd hit his head when he fell, one time. Another time, his car had hit a tree. There were a couple more things like that.'

'Did it seem to you, from what you knew of Jack Burns, that his judgment was impaired?'

'Yes, he . . .' and then I had no excuse to loiter, though I dearly wanted to, because Trinity came out of the reception area and started to go to the doctor's office with some files.

I had more to think about than I could cram in my brain. I'd dropped Angel off at home, promising to take her prescription for maternity vitamins to the pharmacy on my way home from work. Angel clearly wanted some time to herself, and I could understand why. Telling your forty-seven-year-old vasectomied husband that he's about to be a dad was not an enviable proposition. I wanted to talk the situation over with Martin, but of course I couldn't tell him Angel was expecting until she told her own husband. So probably it was just as well I had to go to work.

The Lawrenceton Public Library is a large two-storey block with a low addition to the rear of the building for offices. This brand-new addition, achieved mostly by a bequest from an anonymous patron, a few other donations, and matching community improvement funds, is easily the nicest part of the library, and it's a pity I get to spend so little time in it. It consists of a large employee break room with a row of bright lockers for personal possessions, a microwave, refrigerator, table and chairs, and a stove; Sam Clerrick's office (with space outside for a secretary, though now he only has a volunteer part-time); and a 'community interest' room, where various clubs can meet free of charge if they are careful to schedule it well ahead of time. And there's a nice employee bathroom.

The rest of the library, where I get to spend my working hours, is a plain old creaky public building, with indoor-outdoor carpeting that resembles woven dead grass with trampled-in mustard, the usual row upon row of gray metal shelves, a two-storey entrance and nice staircase up to the second floor, which has a gallery running all the way around with various Dewey Decimal categories lining it, and lots of table-and-chair sets for kids doing homework or genealogists doing research. There's an area set aside by clever use of shelving and extra bulletin boards, and it's designated as the Children's Room.

Whatever its drawbacks, overall there is that wonderful smell of books, and the relaxing, intelligent feeling of being surrounded by generation after generation of thought.

I've got libraries in my blood.

Of course, there are a few things I have to put up with to work in this wonderful place, and one of them was bearing down on me. Lillian Schmidt, buttons bulging and girdle creaking, had her eyebrows up in that 'Hah! I caught you!' look.

'Late today, aren't we?' Lillian fired as her opening shot.

'Yes, I'm afraid so. I had to take a friend to the doctor.'

'Wonder what would happen if all of us did that? Guess the library just wouldn't open!'

I took a deep breath.

'I'm late enough as it is,' I said with a smile. 'Excuse me, Lillian, but I can't stand here and chat.' I pulled out the little key to my locker, used it, and stuck my purse inside, pocketing the key in my khaki slacks. I was due to tell a story in two minutes.

The librarian I was replacing, at least temporarily, was the children's librarian.

Perhaps ten preschoolers were already seated in an expectant semicircle when I plopped down in the big chair in the middle.

'Good morning!' I said with enough glee to raise a hot-air balloon.

'Good morning,' the children chorused back politely. This was the First Church of God the Creator day-care group, with a couple of other loose kids thrown in, story-time regulars. The moms and the daycare providers sat in a little group over in one corner, their expression one of relief that someone else was shouldering the burden, at least for a few minutes.

'This morning, I'm going to tell you about Alexander's bad day,' I said, casting a covert glance at the book the volunteer for the morning, my friend Lizanne Sewell, had left by the chair: *Alexander and the No-Good, Awful, Very Bad*

Day. Most of the kids turned hopeful faces in my direction, though a few were looking anywhere but at me.

'I'll bet some of you have had bad days at one time or another, am I right? What happened on your bad day, Irene?' This to a little girl with a wonderful, large easy-to-read name tag. Irene pushed her shaggy black bangs out of her eyes and squashed the slack in her T-shirt in one grubby fist.

'On my bad day my dad left my mom and me and went to live in Memphis,' Irene said.

I closed my eyes.

It was only ten o'clock in the morning.

'Well, Irene, that *was* a bad day,' I said, nodding soberly to show I was giving due weight to her problem. 'Has anyone else ever had a bad day?' I looked around the circle, hoping no one could top Irene's.

'I knocked over my cereal bowl one day,' offered a little boy the color of ground coffee. I tried not to look relieved. His mother was not so guarded.

'That was a bad day, too,' I acknowledged. 'Now, let me tell you about Alexander's bad day . . . and if you sit still, you can see the pictures in the book as I tell the story.'

Over to one side, Lizanne was shaking her head gently from side to side, her lips pursed to hold in a giggle. Not daring to glance again in her direction, I began the book, one of my favorites.

The rest of the story time went by without a hitch, and most of the children seemed to enjoy it, which was not always the case. Only one had to go to the bathroom, and only two whispered to each other, which was quite good. Irene was one of the day-care children, so her mother wasn't there to upbraid me for traumatizing Irene with my probing interrogation.

'It would be better for Irene if he didn't come back,' one of the day-care workers murmured in my ear as they gathered up their flock to return to the church. 'He drank like a fish.' I thought briefly of Jack Burns driving his car into a tree, then forced myself back to the present.

I realized the woman was trying to make me feel better, and I smiled and thanked her. 'Come back soon, kids!' I chirped, being perky all over the place.

The little ones all smiled and waved, even the ones who hadn't listened to a word I said.

Lizanne was ready to help me change the bulletin board, and in fact she'd made most of the items to go on it. With construction paper and some contact sheets, we'd created butterflies, hummingbirds, fish, books, baseballs, and other signs of warm weather. Maybe we were being unduly optimistic about the books, but the summer reading pro- gram had always been one of the library's best features, and Sam was counting on me to start plugging it early.

After we'd commented on the way story time had gone, Lizanne and I began to work together companionably, referring to our sketch of the finished product from time to time, handing each other push pins or border and so on. From time to time Lizanne would stop and press a hand to her protuberant stomach; the baby was moving a lot, since she was in her sixth month. Every time, Lizanne would smile her beautiful slow smile.

'Has Bubba made plans for what to do if the baby comes while the legislature's in session?' I asked.

'At least ten plans,' Lizanne said. 'But maybe it'll come before he reconvenes.'

Bubba Sewell, Lizanne's husband, was a state representative and a local lawyer. Bubba was ambitious and intelligent, and, I think, basically an honest person. Lizanne was beautiful and slow-moving and somehow almost always managed things so that they pleased her. I could hardly wait to see what the baby's character would be.

Lizanne left to eat lunch with her mother-in-law, to whose opinions on the baby's upbringing she was blandly indifferent, and I helped some preschool children pick out books. One mother of a nine-year-old boy with a stomach bug came in to get some books and videos to keep him amused, and I collected a few natural history books with plenty of gross pictures of frogs and snakes.

My stomach was growling inelegantly at one o'clock when the library aide came to the children's room to take my place. The aide was a heavy woman with pecan-colored skin named Beverly Rillington, who couldn't be more than twenty-one. Whether it was because of race, age, or income level, Beverly and I were having a hard time geeing and hawing together. She and the previous children's librarian had also had personality conflicts, Sam Clerrick had warned me. But Beverly, hired under a job-training program, was efficient and reliable, and Sam had no intention of letting her go.

'How's it going today?' Beverly asked. She looked down at me as though she didn't really want to know.

In an attempt to break the ice, I told Beverly about the morning story hour and the disconcerting answer I'd gotten from Irene.

Beverly looked at me as though I should have known in advance I'd hear more than I bargained for. If Beverly made me anxious, terrified I might step on her many sensitive toes, I clearly waved a red flag in her face just by being who and what I was. Beverly never volunteered anything about her home life and did not respond to references to mine. Making contact with her was one of my projects for the year.

('I'm damned if I know why,' Martin had said simply, when I'd told him.)

As I told Beverly good-bye and prepared to go home to see my husband off and be interviewed by Mr Dryden, I found myself wondering why, too.

But the answer came to me easily enough, in a string of reasons. Beverly was naturally good with kids, any kids, a knack God had left out of my genetic makeup. Beverly was never late and always completed her work, i's dotted and t's crossed. And, oh happy day, Lillian Schmidt was so terrified of Beverly that she avoided the children's area like the plague when Beverly was at work. I owed my aide thanks on many levels, and I was determined to put up with a certain gruffness of manner for those reasons, if no others.

Chapter Three

I'd forgotten Martin had decided to drive to the airport directly from work. He'd leave his Mercedes at the plant and pick it up when he came in three days from now. The higher-ups of Pan-Am Agra had scheduled one of those events that made Martin's blood curdle: a seminar on sexual harassment, recognition and avoidance thereof. All the plant managers were flying in to Chicago to attend, and since Martin had no particular friends among them and hated meetings he wasn't chairing, his most positive attitude was grim acceptance.

When he called me to say he was leaving for the airport, he reminded me over and over about setting the house security system every night. 'How's Angel?' he asked, just when he was about to hang up. 'Shelby said she hadn't been feeling well.'

'Um. We'll talk about it when you get back. She's going to be fine.'

'Roe, tell me. Is she well enough to help you if you have an emergency?'

I was the only librarian in Lawrenceton, quite possibly in all of Georgia – perhaps even America – to have her own bodyguard. I thought of Angel, stunned and scared, in the doctor's office that morning, and I thought of calling her for help. 'Sure, she's okay,' I said reassuringly. 'Oh, by the way,

I saw one of the – well, I don't know exactly who Dryden and O'Riley work for . . . they never said – well, I ran into him this morning, and he says he has to come out here to talk to me this afternoon.'

I'd almost said I'd met him at the doctor's, when I'd taken Angel; and then Martin would have asked what the doctor had said, and I didn't want to lie about it.

'Why does he have to talk to you?' Martin asked.

'To tell you the truth, I'm not sure.'

'Roe, have Angel in the house with you when he's there.'

'Martin, she's not well.'

'Promise.'

Now Martin almost never pulled that string, and it was one we both honored.

'Okay. If she's not actually throwing up, I'll have her here.'

'Good,' he said. 'Now, what can I bring you from Chicago?'

I thought of the big stores, the endless possibilities. I didn't like that many choices myself.

'Surprise me,' I said with a smile he could hear in my voice.

We said some personal good-byes, and then he went back to his work world, which I could hardly imagine.

I piffled around the house for a while, cleaning the downstairs bathroom and sweeping the front porch, the patio, and the steps that led up from the covered walkway running between the garage and the side kitchen door. Finally, I called Angel.

She said dutifully that she'd be over before four o'clock, and I apologized for disturbing her on such a day. 'Martin made me promise,' I explained.

'It's my job,' Angel said. 'Besides, I don't want to just sit here and wait for Shelby to come home.'

The doorbell rang.

'There's a florist's van in the driveway,' Angel said. She must have been on her portable phone, looking out the front window of the garage apartment. 'I'm coming down.'

She hung up unceremoniously, and I went to the front door and turned off the security system. I heard Angel unlocking the side door leading into the kitchen as the doorbell rang a second time. By the time I shot back the dead bolt, she was standing behind me.

'Delivery to this address,' said the young black man in blue coveralls. *DeLane* was stitched on the left chest pocket. He had in his hands a huge arrangement of mixed spring flowers in a tall, clear glass vase. It was lovely: daffodils, baby's breath, irises, roses.

'Who's it for?' I asked.

DeLane looked very uncomfortable. 'It only says, "To the most beautiful". You ladies have to fight over it, I guess,' he added more cheerfully. He'd had a look at Angel, and I could tell he'd decided who would win.

'Who placed the order?' Angel asked sharply.

'We got it Call-a-Posy from Atlanta,' he said with a shrug. 'It seemed pretty strange to us, too, but the shop in Atlanta said it had been paid for. Probably someone'll call you ladies before long, tell you he sent it.'

'Thanks,' Angel said abruptly. She took the vase from his hands.

I said good-bye and shut the door.

Angel was holding the flowers, looking them over carefully. She put them on the low coffee table and peered at the stems through the clear glass; she gently poked the flowers apart with a long finger.

'I don't like things coming without a card, coming "to the most beautiful",' she said. 'That's creepy. Presents without names on them make me very suspicious.'

I wondered if Martin could have sent them, perhaps stopped in at a florist's on his way to the airport. I didn't think so. He knew there were two women at this address, he would have signed a card, it just didn't feel right. And the same thing held true for Shelby, who was much more likely to buy Angel a new running outfit or a punching bag than a huge bouquet of flowers. (For Christmas he'd gotten her a new holster for carrying a concealed gun.)

' "Mirror, mirror, on the wall, Who's the fairest one of all?" ' I quoted, trying to make light of the situation. 'You want to take them home, make Shelby jealous? Or maybe he sent them.'

Angel shook her head morosely. 'Having to answer questions about these flowers would just complicate things even more, and I know damn good and well Shelby didn't send them.'

Our formal dining room lay between the living room and the kitchen, so I went through the large open archway to put a plastic mat in the center of the dining room table. Angel came after me, still frowning, and put the vase on the mat, wiping her hands on her jeans right afterward as if rubbing off the feel of the vase. We both stood and gazed at the flowers some more, but since they didn't suddenly communicate who had sent them, or blow up, or do anything but sit there looking like flowers, this had limited appeal. I was on the verge of suggesting to Angel we go stare at the inside of the refrigerator when the doorbell rang again.

'Oh, gosh, it's four o'clock,' I said, glancing at my wristwatch. 'It must be Dryden and O'Riley.' I looked up at Angel. 'I should be safe with them.' I was smiling, but she was not.

'I said I'd stay.'

'Okay.' I went to the door, my heels making a little click on the polished wood floor, a sound that almost always improved my spirits. My house was now about sixty-three years old, and we'd restored it to wonderful condition. It was just an old family home, not even *my* old family home, but I loved it.

I hadn't reset the alarm system, so Dryden was admitted more rapidly than the florist's deliveryman.

I looked behind him, but O'Riley was nowhere in sight. I was conscious of feeling glad, as I stood aside to let him in, that Angel had decided to stay. At that moment, Dryden's gaze lighted on her, and his mouth yanked up at one corner, an enigmatic twitch I was unable to interpret. It could have been anything from deep admiration for such a fine specimen of womanhood to irritation that I'd asked someone else to sit in on our conversation.

'You're by yourself,' I said, since I've never been afraid to state the obvious.

'O'Riley's on another interview,' he said, pushing his tortoise-shell-rimmed glasses back on his nose. As if the gesture were contagious, like yawning in a meeting, I pushed mine back, too, and we stared at each other solemnly.

'Please have a seat,' I told him. 'This is Angel Youngblood. She was in the backyard when Jack Burns fell, too.'

48

'Thanks for saving us a trip out here,' Dryden said, and I still couldn't read his expression. He must have recognized Angel as the woman with me in Dr Zelman's office in the morning. He must have read all the police reports, and must have known already about Angel's presence during the free fall of Jack Burns. Yet he didn't seem interested.

I was getting more and more confused by John Dryden.

He finally sat on the couch, and Angel and I picked single chairs opposite him. He turned down my ritual offer of coffee or iced tea, though it was a warm day outside and his suit jacket must be hot.

I looked at Dryden closely for the first time. He was big, and square-shouldered, and husky, but not fat, not at all. His eyes were blue behind the glasses, and if he had any gray hair, his light blond hair color concealed it. Of course it was cut very short, as I'd always been led to believe FBI agents wore their hair – if he was an FBI agent – and it lay on his head as smooth as polish. The only other man I knew with hair that blond was Detective Arthur Smith, once my significant other, now married and a father. Lately when I'd run across Arthur his eyes had been hungry. Suddenly I wondered if he'd sent the flowers.

I guess I got lost in conjecture, for a loud throat-clearing brought me back to the here and now with a jolt. Angel and Dryden were both waiting for me to say something.

I sighed. 'Excuse me, I wasn't paying attention. Could you repeat that?'

'Do you know how to fly an airplane?'

I laughed at the idea. 'No,' I said, since he obviously wanted an answer on the record. 'I don't think I've ever been in the cockpit of a plane.'

'What about you, Mrs Youngblood?'

'I had a few flying lessons in Florida,' she said calmly. I noticed Angel's long fingers were resting across her flat stomach. It was incredible to me that a child could be in such a small space, invisible and unknown to anyone around Angel. What an amazing thing to carry inside you; the other choices were so mundane or deathly, like a cold, or cancer, or appendicitis . . .

I had been drifting again.

'. . . you remember the name of your instructor?'

'Bunny Black. She was the owner of this little flying school, Daredevil . . . but we had to move and I never had another chance to get my pilot's license.'

Dryden was jotting all this down, which was plain ridiculous, since Angel had been standing, both feet very much on the ground, while the plane had been absolutely up in the sky.

I said as much, politely.

He shrugged, and continued to scribble.

If he was this exasperating at home, his wife would take a meat cleaver to him one of these days. I leaned over slightly to check his left hand. No ring. Well, I wasn't surprised.

Suddenly he looked up from his notebook, his eyes unexpectedly sharp and blue. We stared at each other for what seemed like a very long moment.

I eased back against the chair with an uneasy feeling I'd just contacted Mars.

We continued trolling drearily over the horror of yesterday, with Angel and me unable to add a scintilla of information to what we'd already told the county people. I began to be sorry I couldn't suddenly recall some amazing fact to tell him. 'I just remembered! I had a camera in my hand and I think I clicked the button just as the pilot leaned out of the window of the plane!' I bet *that* would change the expression on Dryden's face . . .

Shoot, I'd done it again.

'About your relationship with Jack Burns, Ms Teagarden . . .' Dryden was saying, and I snapped to attention in a very big hurry.

I couldn't help glancing over at Angel. Her eyes narrowed, she was looking at Dryden carefully, as if deciding where her first blow would fall.

'I never had a relationship with Jack Burns,' I said flatly.

'So it's not true that he expressed hostility to you publicly on at least two occasions?'

'I didn't count,' I said flippantly, and was instantly sorry. 'Truly, Mr Dryden,' and I abruptly remembered police remarking in some article I'd read that suspects invariably were lying when they prefaced a statement with 'To tell the truth,' or 'Honestly'. 'To the best of my recollection, Mr Dryden, I hadn't spoken to Jack Burns in over two years, so I don't think you can say that we had a relationship.' Jack Burns had just seen me in the vicinity of too many corpses to suit his strong police sense. He'd felt I just about had to be guilty of *something*.

But I didn't want to try to explain this. And I didn't feel I should have to.

'Mrs Youngblood, you live in the garage apartment over there?' Dryden pointed with his pencil to the garage, clearly visible out the south windows of the living room.

Angel nodded.

'You rent from Ms Teagarden here?'

'We live there rent-free in return for helping Roe and Martin.' Angel looked completely relaxed, completely blank. She just almost wasn't there at all.

'Helping?'

Angel raised her eyebrows very slightly. 'We help with the yardwork, I help Roe with her housework, we do all the things you need an extra person to do. Martin travels a lot, and it works out conveniently for Roe.'

I would like to see the day I asked Angel to help me with my housework. But a realistic answer – 'We're bodyguards' – would require a lot more explanation than either of us wanted to give.

'And this working relationship has existed for how long?'

'Oh, come on, what possible bearing can this have on Jack Burns being murdered?' I asked, suddenly sick and tired of the presence of Dryden in my house, the boredom of these interminable and uncomfortable questions. I could think of lots of things I needed to be doing and would rather be doing than this. And Angel's husband would be home in about ten minutes, and she should be preparing for a tense and critical evening.

I rose to my feet.

'Mr Dryden, I don't mean to be rude,' though I suppose I really did, 'but I assume you have better things to do than this. And I know I do. All we did was be absolutely random witnesses to this terrible thing.'

Dryden, his mouth flattened in anger – at least, I thought it was anger – was putting away his pencil and notebook.

'I hope it won't be necessary to disturb you again,' he said, quite calmly. He looked over my shoulder, through the archway to the dining room. 'Pretty flowers,' he said, still without inflection.

'Thanks for coming,' I said, with, I hoped, firm civility.

Angel looked down at me, shaking her head, when he'd left.

'What?' I asked indignantly.

'When you do that, it's just like being bitten by a dachshund,' she said, and drifted to the kitchen door. 'Don't forget to set the alarm after me,' she called over her shoulder. I watched her through the kitchen window, loping across the covered sidewalk to the garage, bounding up the wooden steps and unlocking her door. I obediently punched in the right numbers on the panel set in the wall, and I prayed for her and Shelby and the baby.

That evening I got another one of those annoying phone calls. I'd been getting quite a few lately, the wrong numbers that don't say anything when an unfamiliar voice answers the phone. The least the caller could do is say, 'Excuse me, wrong number,' or 'I'm sorry to bother you.' Finally I let it ring until the answering machine picked up. So of course, my next caller was Martin. I just let him assume I'd been too far from the phone to pick it up on the first three rings; no point in telling him about the hang-ups. He'd just worry, maybe call the Youngbloods and get them to worry, too.

I didn't tell him about the flowers, either.

I didn't tell him about Angel's pregnancy.

I did tell him about my interview with Dryden. When Martin realized Dryden had come alone, he did one of the things that made me love him; he didn't say one word about his foresight in insisting Angel be present. But I could hear the difference in his voice as we talked; there was the steel there, the hardness and the edge, that I seldom heard. Maybe that was how he was at work all day, and didn't bring it home; or maybe only danger brought it out, some perceived threat to him and those people or things he held dear.

And you couldn't accuse him of paranoia, of being too cautious; not with the things I heard on the news every day, not with the horrors he'd seen in Vietnam and Central America. It would be insane egocentrism for me to believe none of these horrors could happen to me.

From far away in Chicago, a city I'd never visited, Martin told me to use my common sense, and for God's sake to remember to set the security system.

Chapter Four

Madeleine had jumped on the bed in the middle of the night. She was there, curled in a large golden ball, when I woke up. Madeleine was an older cat now; she'd been at least six when I'd inherited her, and Jane Engle, her first owner, had now been dead for about three years. Madeleine still managed to catch the occasional mouse or bird, but she sometimes missed her jumps, and her facial fur seemed whiter to me. The vet gave her high marks on her annual checkups, and since everyone at his office would have loved to find an excuse to put Madeleine to sleep, I had to accept his verdict.

Now she purred in a rusty way as I scratched behind her ears. Martin hated Madeleine getting on the bed, so she only got to stay there when he was gone; I vacuumed or washed the bedspread before he came home. As my fingers tickled lower on her neck, they encountered something unfamiliar.

I sat up and really looked at Madeleine for the first time. In addition to her brown leather collar to which were attached her rabies disc and her name-and-address tag, something else had been tied around the cat's neck. It was a ribbon, a fresh-looking pink satin ribbon, tied in a precise, perky bow.

I tried to come up with a reasonable explanation for the bow. It was ludicrous that something as pretty as a pink bow could frighten me.

I looked at the clock. The Youngbloods would be up. I punched in their number on the bed-table phone.

'Yep,' said Shelby flatly.

'I'm sorry to call you this early in the morning. But unless you or Angel did this, and frankly I can't see how or why you would, someone caught Madeleine and got her to hold still while he tied a ribbon around her neck.'

'Run that by again.'

'A man or woman. Got hold of Madeleine the cat. And tied a pink ribbon. Around Madeleine's neck.'

'Why the hell would anyone do that? That cat would as soon dismember you as look at you.'

'Did Angel tell you about the flowers?'

'No.'

Then I remembered they'd had more important things to talk about the night before.

'Someone ordered flowers delivered to this address yesterday. The card was unsigned.' I told Shelby what the card had said. 'Either your wife or I have an unknown admirer. This is unsettling.'

'I'll be over there soon.'

'To do what? Look at the ribbon? What good would that do?'

Shelby was silent for a minute.

'I'll take the cat to the vet this morning,' he said. 'He needs to draw some blood to find out if she was drugged. And I do want a look at the ribbon. We need to keep it, in case we have to call the police.'

'Okay. I'll cut it off with scissors.'

'Then I'll come to get her in about ten minutes.'

Very casually, so as not to alert Madeleine, I got my

fingernail scissors from my vanity table. I began scratching her gently behind the ears again, and she stretched her neck and purred. Then I scratched her forehead, so she'd shut her eyes. Gently, gently, I slid the thin blade of the scissors under the pink band, and just as gently I closed the blades together. Of course, the little snick of the scissors and the feeling of release brought Madeleine's head up with a snap and she bit the hell out of me. I'd expected it; Madeleine had never been a cat who'd known tolerance or temperance, and most often she was a sorry pet indeed.

After I'd sworn a little and put antiseptic on my wound, I wrapped my robe around me and retrieved the cat carrier from its storage in a downstairs closet. Right on time, Shelby knocked on the kitchen door.

I punched in the code to deactivate the alarm and let Shelby in. Shelby, so tall and pockmarked and grim, can be intimidating. I had come to be at ease with Angel, but Shelby still made me a little anxious.

This morning was different.

'Roe, you got time to talk?' he asked quietly.

I glanced at the clock. I didn't have to be at the library for an hour.

'Sure,' I said. 'Want some coffee?'

He shook his head. 'Roe,' he said directly while I poured a cup of my own, 'have you ever seen anyone out here when I was gone?'

I set my coffee down with a thunk, walked over to Shelby Youngblood, and slapped the tar out of him. I was so mad I couldn't talk for a second.

'Don't you ever ever imply that your wife has been unfaithful to you!' I told him. 'If you had been there in that

57

doctor's office yesterday and seen how upset she was, if you had seen how scared she was you wouldn't believe her, you would *never* say a stupid thing like that.'

And then I realized Shelby wasn't the only one saying and doing stupid things. I had just slapped someone who could snap my neck quicker than I could picture him doing it.

'So you believe what this doctor says?' Shelby asked in a controlled, reasonable voice.

'Sure I do. You know Angel. You and she are just like male and female halves of the same thing.'

'But that female half is pregnant and that male half had a vasectomy.'

'So go get tested,' I challenged him. 'Would you rather go' – and here I was stuck for a moment over how to put it – 'put a specimen in a jar at the doctor's, or would you rather believe your wife cheated on you?'

'Put that way . . .' he said, and to my amazement he hugged me.

It was then that I learned a lesson about the vagaries of chemistry. I loved Martin, and Shelby loved Angel. But for a moment, something crackled in my quiet morning kitchen, and I was very conscious that my breasts were not tucked in a bra. I looked up at Shelby and saw his eyes darken, before the current of electricity reversed and we flew apart.

If we didn't acknowledge it, it would be even worse.

'We'd better not do that again,' I said weakly, and found I needed to clear my throat. I turned away and took a swallow of coffee.

Shelby was silent. I peeked at him and saw he was still in the same spot, his arms still out a little. 'Shelby?' I said anxiously.

He jumped. 'Right,' he said, doing a little swallowing of his own. 'Martin would kill you and Angel would sure kill me, and we'd deserve it.'

I drew my cloak of niceness back around me. I had never wanted to be one of those people I'd secretly scorned, people who could not keep their promises.

'We'd better hurry,' I said briskly. 'I've got to get to work and you know how long it can take to catch Madeleine.'

The decoration of Madeleine proved to be a strange start to a strange day. Every staff member at the library had gotten out of bed on the wrong side, even Sam Clerrick. As Sam hopped all over Lillian Schmidt for speaking sharply to a patron the day before – we could hear his voice in his office as we put our things away in the lockers – I raised my eyebrows significantly at Perry Allison. He rolled his eyes in the direction of the office, in a what-are-you-gonna-do gesture.

Perry, the only child of Sally Allison, had worked at the library before, about three years ago. Overwhelming emotional problems and some substance abuse had put him in a hospital and then an outpatient home in Atlanta, where he'd flourished. After long thought and much negotiation, Sam had agreed to rehire Perry on a provisional basis.

Perry had terrified me before, but now I tended to think his time in the hospital and in the home had been time well spent. Perry, who was my age, seemed to be on an even keel and well in control of himself. Perry had dark hair, which he wore in a fashionable brush cut on top and rather longer on the sides and back. He had brown eyes, like his mother, and they were magnified by the aviator-style wire-rims he affected. Though he was weedy in build, Perry always looked good in the starched shirts and bright silk ties he regarded as his work uniform.

As we both shut our lockers and tried not to listen too obviously to Sam's high voice, I realized that I'd accepted Perry with few reservations. At first it'd been hard, working with someone I used to be frightened of; I'd been tense every day. Now, I almost took him for granted.

'Who'd Lillian offend?' I whispered.

'Cile Vernon. You didn't hear?'

I shook my head, pouring myself a cup of coffee from the staff pot. It had been Lillian's morning to make it, and whatever her other faults, she made good coffee.

'Cile wanted to check out one of Anne Rice's witch books, and Lillian told her she wouldn't like them, they were full of witchcraft and sex, and Cile said she was sixty-two, she ought to be able to read whatever the hell she wanted.'

'She did not!'

'Yep, she did. And then she marched into Sam's office and said for a librarian to comment on what a reader checked out was tantamount to censorship.'

'Sam waited all this time to talk to Lillian about it?'

'He had to go yesterday afternoon, after you got off work. He and Marva went to help Bess Burns pick out Jack's coffin.'

'The kids haven't gotten in yet?'

'They'd just gotten in, they were wiped out. I hear they're furious someone killed Jack, but not exactly devastated with grief that he's gone. I hear he'd been drinking a lot.'

I thought about the mooshy feelings I'd been having over Angel's pregnancy, and I realized I was seeing the flip side of the coin. Children and parents didn't always have close and loving relationships. Like marriages, the pairing of parents and offspring sometimes didn't work out.

As I went to my desk in the children's area, I reminded myself forcefully that bearing a healthy child didn't mean you lived happily ever after.

Then I saw my aide Beverly, remembered this was the morning we worked together, and felt my day take another downturn. Fixing a pleasant smile on my face, I sat at my desk.

Beverly was shelving books and muttering to herself. This was one of Beverly's most irritating habits, especially since I was almost sure she was saying unflattering things about me just low enough for me to miss. Despite my mental recital of her good qualities only the day before, I felt my heart sink at the prospect of trying to deal with the woman. That chip on her shoulder was the size of Stone Mountain, and everything you asked of her, everything you said or did, had to be filtered through Beverly's resentment.

Feeling the familiar twinges of guilt, I recited my comforting mantra to myself: I was as glad to see black library patrons as white, I thought black kids were as cute as white kids, I worked as well with black librarians as white. Except Beverly Rillington.

Still, there were days when Beverly would just do her work and I'd just do mine, and I'd hoped fervently this would be one of those days.

But it wasn't.

I could hear the book cart slamming into corners as she

rolled it along from shelf to shelf. The muttering faded and grew stronger as she turned from the cart to the shelf, then back to the cart. I couldn't quite make it out, of course, but I had a stronger-than-ever feeling it had to do with my faults.

I sighed and unlocked the desk to get out my scheduling notebook. I had two telephone message slips waiting on the blotter, and they both contained requests for special story-telling times for a couple of daycare centers. WeeOnes had asked for the time I'd slotted for another group; I searched the appointment book and made a note of two different times it would be convenient for them to come. Kid Kare Korner wanted to come in the afternoon; that would be feasible only if I stayed late or if Beverly were willing to do the story hour.

I sighed again. Getting to be a habit.

It would almost be better to work late without getting paid for it than to ask Beverly to do a story time. She violently resented being asked to do it, but she was offended if you didn't ask. In a cowardly way, I put off making a decision, and began to work on the list of suggested books one of the kindergarten teachers had asked me to prepare. I'd gone over the list compiled by the previous children's librarian and taken a dislike to a few of the books she routinely recommended, so when a new list had become necessary I'd found myself combing the shelves. I had a pile on the table in front of me I'd been reading, and I picked up the top one to whittle down my stack still further.

'Some of us have to come in here and really *work*, not just sit at a damn desk,' the muttering resumed, suddenly quite clear.

I clenched my hands. I read another page. If the children's

area had been a real room, instead of a corner of the ground floor, I would have shut the door and had a discussion with Beverly. As it was, I could just hope to ignore her until I could talk to her away from the patrons. There weren't many, but there were some; I saw Arthur Smith waiting impatiently at the checkout desk while Lillian put a pile of children's videos into a bag, and Sally had come in and was talking to Perry in a hushed tone by the water fountain. A youngish man I didn't know was browsing through the new books shelved close to the entrance, and it occurred to me that he'd been there an awfully long time.

To my surprise, Angel came in the double front doors, dressed quietly in blue jeans and a striped T-shirt. She was carrying a shopping bag from Marcus Hatfield and a gift-wrapped box. I didn't recall Angel ever coming all the way inside the library before, and she was looking around now curiously, her head turning smoothly from side to side like a large cat surveying a new territory.

She spied me and came toward me just as the volcano that was Beverly Rillington erupted.

'Does just one of us work here?' Beverly asked venomously, approaching me from the left side.

'What?' I could not believe I was hearing her correctly, and her stance was even more threatening. Beverly was too close, her hands clenched, leaning forward, aggression in every line of her body. Beverly had never been pleasant, but she was obviously under a stress so extreme she had lost all judgment.

I was afraid that if I stood up Beverly would actually hit me, so I stayed in my chair at the low desk with the open book in one hand. Angel, who was approaching Beverly from the side, had quietly put down the bag and box. I suddenly knew I couldn't bear it if Angel defended me here in the library, my own stomping ground.

'Beverly,' I said very quietly, aware that Perry and Sally had looked over curiously. Well, just about everyone was looking over. 'Beverly, you are mad at me, but let's not work it out here. We can go in the staff room or Sam's office.'

'All you have to do is do your damn job,' Beverly hissed. 'You're sitting on your butt doing nothing, I'm doing all the work.'

There's very little point carrying on a conversation with someone who is absolutely convinced you are wrong and bad. Instead of thinking of strategies I found myself speculating, not for the first time, on Beverly's mental health. But I had to defuse the situation somehow; Angel's face had gone blank and she was concentrating on Beverly as a target. If Beverly took one step closer to me, Angel would hit her. And then where would we be?

'Maybe you're right,' I said. 'Maybe you've been doing too much of the work and I haven't been pulling my share. Why don't we talk to Sam about it?'

'He'll just side with you,' Beverly said, but there wasn't quite as much repressed fury in her voice as before.

'I'll call him right now,' I said, and lifted the phone and punched in the correct numbers.

'Sam,' I said briskly when he picked up the receiver, 'Beverly and I are having some problems working together. Beverly feels she's carrying too heavy a load.'

'She does,' Sam said thoughtfully. I heard his chair creak

as he leaned back. 'It has been more work for her, not having a full-time librarian in that section.'

'We'd better make an appointment to meet with you and discuss it,' I said very evenly. 'In *your office.*'

'Roe, do you have a situation out there?'

'As soon as possible,' I said, so calmly I could have been discussing spraying the roses for aphids.

'Right. I gotcha. Okay, then, one o'clock today when you get off.'

'That's fine. I'll tell her.'

'We're to meet in his office at one o'clock,' I told Beverly, putting the phone down very gently. To my relief, her posture was less aggressive. Sally had gone back to talking to her son, but Perry's eyes remained on us watchfully. Arthur was browsing through the new books, though he'd completed checking out the videos. A couple of other patrons who had tried to listen without showing overt attention, courteous Southerners that they were, went back to their activities with some relief.

Beverly turned to resume work, I thought, and spotted Angel. 'Whatchu lookin' at?' Beverly snarled, in an exaggerated street drawl. The two women stared at each other for a long minute. But even Beverly had to concede defeat against Angel, and with a 'Humph!' to show contempt and save face, Beverly returned to her book cart.

I bent back over the book on my desk and put my hands down in my lap to hide their shaking. Tears stung my eyes. Things happening in public were so much worse than things happening in private, and if anything had happened in the library . . . if it had come to blows between Angel and Beverly . . . in the *library!*

Oh, I just hated for people to see me cry. And of course there weren't any Kleenex in my desk drawer. A crying child had used the last one two days ago and I'd forgotten to restock. Hellfire and damnation.

A hand appeared under my nose, a white cotton handkerchief in it. The hand dropped the handkerchief on the desk, and I swooped it up gratefully and applied it to my dripping eyes and nose.

'Thanks, Arthur,' I said in the clogged voice that is one of the more attractive features of crying.

'Don't mention it,' he said. 'How'd you know it was me?'

'I remember your hands,' I said without thinking.

I looked up in horror when I realized what I'd said, and saw that Arthur's face was slowly flushing red, as it always had when he . . . well, when we had personal moments.

If today got any better, I'd just spend tomorrow locked in the attic of my house. It'd be a safer place.

Angel was standing at a discreet distance, her eyes on Beverly, who had gone back to shelving books. At the front desk, Lillian was now eyeing Arthur and me with avid curiosity. Sally was gone, and Perry was watering the large, ugly potted plant (I am not an indoor plant person) that flanked the double main doors.

Arthur slowly returned to his normal coloring, said 'Good-bye' in a rough voice, and left. The water in the plant overflowed into the large dish the pot sits in. Lillian bent down to get a book from below the counter to hand to the young man, and Angel handed me the gift-wrapped package.

It was as if someone had changed channels on a

television. Suddenly, everything was back to normal. The Beverly incident might not have happened.

'It's for you, for taking me to the doctor yesterday. And I don't know what you said to Shelby, but suddenly he seems okay about this. Who's the bitch over there?'

'Thanks for the gift. Shelby loves you. Beverly Rillington.'

'What's her problem?'

'I'll tell you later,' I said quietly, hoping Beverly wasn't listening. 'Can I open my present now?' I tried to scrape up a smile that would pass for normal.

'Sure,' Angel said. 'Guess what I've got in my shopping bag.'

Angel was being a will-o'-the-wisp today. Generally, I'd found Angel to be a very thorough, slow worker, unless you were in her professional field, martial arts and protection services. Then she was quick and lethal.

Now, this quick, lethal woman had bought me a golden brown silk blouse that I thought was perfectly lovely.

I told her so.

'It looked like something you would wear,' she said shyly. 'Is that the right size?'

'Yes,' I said happily. 'Thanks a lot, Angel. I hope you bought yourself something?'

Angel looked proudly embarrassed. From her Marcus Hatfield bag she pulled a maternity T-shirt in white and blue, a white maternity blouse, and a black jumper.

'Oh, they're pretty. Are pants going to be a problem?'

'Sure are,' she said, perching on the edge of my desk and refolding her purchases. 'I'm too tall for all the pants and about four fifths of the dresses I tried on. This jumper'll have to do.'

'You need a dress soon?' I asked. I'd never known Angel to wear a dress.

'Yes. The funeral,' she explained. 'Jack Burns. You know?' And she made a graphic tumbling motion with her long thin hand, culminating in a splat on the surface of my desk.

'When is it?'

'Within a week. They'll have the body back by then.'

'And you're going?'

'I feel like I ought to, somehow,' Angel said. 'I knew him, too. You know, besides the ticket thing.'

I tried not to stare. 'No. I didn't know that.'

'He had started coming to the Athletic Club in the evenings, getting on the treadmill. He knew I lived out by you.'

'He talked about me?'

'Yeah,' she said casually, slipping her hand through the plastic grips of the shopping bag. 'He had a bee in his bonnet about you, Roe. Well, see ya later.' And she strode out, golden and tall and lean, and for the first time since I'd met her, radiantly happy.

Chapter Five

When I came in to work the next morning, I was not feeling exactly cheerful. The discussion with Sam the day before had gone about as I'd expected it to go, Beverly stoutly denying she was difficult to work with, accusing me of many things, all but saying that had she had my education she would now have my job. That may have been true, but it was not the issue we were there to discuss. Even if I'd agreed with that assumption, it wouldn't have changed a thing.

After an upsetting forty-five minutes, during which nothing had been settled and Sam's hair had turned a little grayer right before my eyes, I'd gone to pick up Madeleine at the vet. They'd gotten the blood sample and sent it to a lab, Dr Jamerson had told me with determined cheerfulness, and he expected to get a reply from the lab in a few days, maybe a week. I'd loaded Madeleine in my car with the strong feeling that the vet and his staff wouldn't have minded a bit if the hypothetical drugger had used something stronger and more lethal, or perhaps tied that bow a little tighter.

Somehow I'd expected Dr Jamerson to have the answer ready right then – had Madeleine been drugged or had she not? – and not knowing had thrown me even further off course. As Madeleine yowled on the way home, I had found myself thinking of getting a dog, a medium-sized stupid one who was everyone's friend. A mutt with brown rough hair and a black muzzle . . . but Jane Engle, who'd left me Madeleine and a heck of a lot of money, had somehow astral-projected her strongly disapproving face right into my consciousness.

So I trudged into the library's back door feeling dispirited. At least Angel had been out running this morning as I was driving in to town. She'd grinned and waved at me. A smiling Angel – and one with a bulging abdomen – was something I would have to get used to. I smoothed my own oversized orange T-shirt over my stomach; I was wearing orange leggings, too, and there was a big gold sun on the front of my tee. I was hoping the children would think it a cheerful outfit. I'd pulled my hair back with an orange-and-gold barrette, and I was wearing my gold-framed glasses. Just a blaze of color, that was me.

'Who was that woman who came in to see you yesterday?' Perry asked, as I stowed my purse in my locker. He was using the microwave to make hot chocolate, which he drank regardless of the outside temperature; he had quite a sweet tooth, though by his leanness you wouldn't have guessed it.

Here I was, I thought wryly, glowing all over the place, and as usual, I was being asked about . . . my bodyguard.

'Angel Youngblood.'

'She's not local.'

'No. She's from Florida.'

'Married?'

Well, well, well. 'Very,' I said firmly. 'And a black belt in karate, as is her husband.'

70

Perry didn't seem dismayed by this news. 'She's just stunning,' he said. 'I could tell by the way she walks that she's an athlete. And her coloring is so unusual.'

'Yep, she's gold,' I answered, burrowing in my locker for a tube of breath mints. I'd had this conversation with many men (and some women) about Angel. 'I thought you were pretty tight with Jenny Tankersley?'

'Oh, we're dating,' Perry said casually, though his mother Sally had told me they were all but engaged.

Jenny wouldn't have been pleased to hear Perry dismiss her so cavalierly, from what I'd heard of her. She'd been married for a few years to a man who ran his own crop-dusting service, and when Jack Tankersley had made a fatal mistake regarding plane altitude one summer, Jenny had ended up selling the business and doing very well for herself. She'd stayed on as general dogsbody for the three pilots who'd bought it, doing every task from answering the phone to ordering supplies to making out the cheques, and occasionally she flew herself, as she had with her husband.

Perry seemed drawn to strong women.

'Your friend Angel must be the woman Paul was talking about last night,' Perry said, stirring his Swiss Miss with a plastic spoon. I was standing awkwardly, my weight on the foot closest to the door, waiting to terminate this conversation so I could get to my area, though I was dreading seeing Beverly. I had a kindergarten class coming in fifteen minutes, and I'd left a note requesting yesterday's volunteer to cut out twenty-two spring flowers, one for each child to write his or her name on, to stick to the ends of the bookshelves. Hopefully, each child would bring a parent into the library to see the flower, and the child and the parent would both check out books. I had to get out the yellow stickum, and I had to count the flowers . . .

'You had supper with your mom's ex?' I said with some surprise.

'Paul and I have always gotten along. He's been more like a father than an uncle to me. Especially since I've only seen Dad a few times in my whole life,' Perry added with understandable bitterness.

The fact that Sally's latest ex, Paul Allison, was the brother of Sally's first ex, Perry's father Steve, made the situation a little complicated emotionally. I was glad there wasn't a third Allison brother, and I was willing to bet Sally was too.

'Jenny's giving flying lessons now,' Perry said, determined to chat. 'I'm taking, and so is Paul, and your friend Arthur Smith . . .'

'That's great, Perry, and I want to hear more about it later,' I said insincerely. 'I've got to get to work now, I've got a group coming in.'

But even as I banished visions of the Lawrenceton police force on air patrol, focusing instead on visions of little kids who were going to want some individual recognition in about ten minutes, Sam came out of his office and strode over to us looking very worried. Sam is not very good with people; he is a great manager of things, but not a great personnel guy. He's become aware of that in the past few years, and whenever he has to say anything that is going to upset someone, he stews over it.

That's why I didn't expect anything awful; he was probably going to tell me the board had decided to hire a full-time children's librarian and my job was terminated. I had a moment to think of this before he put his hand on my arm and said, 'In view of our conference yesterday, I don't know how you're going to take this, but Beverly Rillington was so badly beaten last night they don't know if she'll live.'

'What? Why?' I asked.

'Sit down, Roe, you're white as a sheet,' Sam advised. He pulled out one of the chairs that had been tucked under the round table.

Perry sat down right by me, and I noticed he was on the pale side, too.

'Beverly's mother Selena was hit by a drunk driver a month ago,' Sam said. 'She's still in a coma at the hospital. Beverly goes to see her every night. When Beverly got out of her car at her house after visiting her mother, someone jumped on her from behind and hit her with a piece of pipe. More than once.'

'Oh my God,' I said. I shook my head. What a dreadful thing. 'Sam, did you know about her mother?' Beverly hadn't breathed a word to me, and I suddenly realized the pressure Beverly had been under. Had pride kept her silent?

'She didn't tell anyone here,' Sam said, shaking his head.

'It was in the paper,' Perry volunteered. 'The wreck, that is. But I didn't realize the injured woman was Beverly's mom.'

'So . . . is Beverly . . . how bad is it?' I asked.

'Severe head wounds,' Sam answered succinctly. 'Listen, I've got to tell the others, and send a flower arrangement to the hospital; don't you have a group coming in this morning, Roe?'

I glanced at my watch and shot out of the chair.

Five minutes later, I met the kindergarten class at the door with a shaky smile, and hoped they wouldn't notice my hands were trembling as I passed each of them a bright construction paper flower.

After they'd left, I had a little time to think between helping patrons. I wondered if someone had it in for Beverly's family. Had her mother's accident really been an accident? Or was the attack on Beverly totally unrelated, a kid on some kind of high taking the easiest money available?

A person would definitely have to be chemically altered to have the nerve to tackle Beverly, who was physically as well as mentally formidable. As I sat with my hands folded in my lap at my little desk, staring blankly at the shelves of books that walled me in, I wished Beverly and I hadn't had our fracas the day before – and when I thought twice about it, I wished even more it hadn't been witnessed by so many people.

Sure enough, when I was called to the phone, Arthur Smith was on the other end, at the police station. The Rillingtons' house was in the city limits, so the city police were handling the investigation into the attack on Beverly.

'Roe, I wonder if I could talk to you after you get off work, about that incident in the library yesterday,' Arthur said. He had always been blunt. Once upon a time, I'd found that directness very exciting.

'Okay,' I said with a detectable lack of enthusiasm.

'Could you come by the station this afternoon, say around two o'clock?'

'I guess so. Why the station?'

'It'll just be more convenient,' he said.

I liked this less and less. But it seemed paranoid to

wonder if I needed a lawyer. Why was Arthur calling me, anyway? He was a robbery detective. Lynn Liggett Smith, his wife, was the only homicide detective on the Lawrenceton force, so other detectives were detailed to her sometimes, but why Arthur?

I began to wonder if I shouldn't call Martin out of his seminar in Chicago and ask his advice. Nah. I'd talk to him tonight. Then I wondered if I should call my mother, and it didn't seem like such a bad idea to tell her where I was going. Naturally, since Mother owns a prosperous realty business, the line was busy. So I figured I'd just stop by on my way to the police station.

Mother's office, established in an old house and redecorated in calm, elegant colors, always made me feel inadequate. I'd hoped once to get interested in real estate, had even started studying for my license, but at last I'd had to admit that my only interest in real estate was in buying my own. When terms like 'equity' and 'Fannie Mae' and 'assumable mortgage' began to be bandied about, my brain glazed over. But when I watched the controlled and purposeful bustle on good days at Select Realty, I felt a pang of regret.

Mother's terrifyingly perfect receptionist, Patty Cloud, had graduated to office manager and then to Realtor. Her understudy, Debbie Lincoln, now controlled the desk in the reception area. Debbie had done some evolving of her own, from a rather slow, silent girl with cornrowed hair and baby fat to a slim, streamlined, fashionable babe who'd become the office computer expert. In the process, Debbie had gained a lot of artifice, and shed some of her natural charm. She'd also acquired confidence and lost her diffidence around older people.

As I entered, she gave me an 'I see you but I'm in the middle of this' smile and waggle of magenta fingernails, the phone clamped between ear and shoulder, her fingers busy separating computer sheets, collating and stapling them.

'Uh-huh. Yes, Mrs Kaplan, she'll be there at three. No, ma'am, you don't need to do anything special. She'll just look over the house and tell you what she'd recommend you ask for it . . . no, ma'am, that doesn't obligate . . . no, ma'am, you can call in as many as you like, but we hope you'll list your house with us . . . right, three o'clock.' Debbie blew a breath out after she'd hung up.

'Difficult?' I asked.

'Girl, you know it,' Debbie said, shaking her head. 'I half hope that woman doesn't decide to list with us. Dealing with her is almost more trouble than it's worth. Your mom is showing a house now, so if you wanted to see her, you may have quite a wait.'

'Heck,' I said. I wondered whether I should leave a note. 'Debbie, do you know Beverly Rillington?' I asked out of the blue.

'Oh, isn't that terrible, what happened to her?' Debbie stapled the last batch of papers together and tossed the result into Eileen Norris's basket, which was half full of phone message slips already. Debbie followed my glance. 'Eileen can't get used to coming out here every time she comes back in the building,' Debbie said. 'So her stuff kind of piles up. I don't really know Beverly that well, she goes to a different church,' she added. 'But Beverly has always been a real tough individual, a real loner. She had a baby, you know, when she was just fourteen . . . and then, when that baby was about a year old, it choked on a marble or something and died. Beverly hasn't had it easy.'

I tried to imagine being pregnant at fourteen. I tried to imagine my baby dying.

I found I didn't want to imagine that.

'I guess I'll just leave Mother a note,' I told her, and started down the hall to Mother's office. It was the biggest one, of course, and Mother had decorated it in cool, elegant gray, with a slash of deep red here and there for eye relief. Her desk was absolutely orderly, though covered with the paperwork on various projects, and I knew the notepads would be in the top right drawer – and they were – and that all Mother's pencils would be sharp . . . and that I would snap off the point of the first one since it was so sharp and I pressed so hard. Having gone through that little ritual, all I had to do was compose a message to let her know I was going to be at the police station at a detective's request, without propelling her out the office door with her flags flying.

Maybe such a composition wasn't possible, I decided after sitting for several blank seconds with the (now blunt) pencil actually resting on the paper.

After a false start or two, I settled on: 'Mom, I'm going to the police station to tell them about working with Beverly Rillington at the library. She got hurt last night. Call me at home at four o'clock. Love, Roe.'

That should do it. I knew if I wasn't at home at four she'd storm the bastions and get me released.

The car by which I parked at the police station/small claims court/county sheriff's office/jail (known locally as

'Spacolec' for *Sperling County Law Enforcement Complex*)
seemed very familiar, and after a second I recognized Angel's
car, the one Jack Burns had ticketed. Then I recalled Angel
telling me she was going to the funeral because they'd
worked out together; the two stories seemed mutually exclusive.

I mulled it over for a minute as I trudged through the hot
parking lot to the glass double doors leading into Spacolec.

It was still making no sense when I saw Arthur Smith
waiting for me right in front of the wall-to-wall admissions
desk. Arthur had changed little in the three years he'd been
married to Lynn. Marriage had not put a gut on him or
lined his face; fatherhood hadn't grayed his tightly curled
hair, though it was such a pale blond that the gray, when it
did appear, would be enviably hard to detect.

Perhaps he'd changed in the way he held himself, his
basic attitude; he seemed tougher, angrier, more impatient,
and that was so apparent that I wondered I hadn't noticed it
before.

Arthur, who'd been chatting with the duty officer, turned
at the hissing sound of the pneumatic doors; He looked at
me, and his face changed.

I felt acutely uncomfortable. I was unused to being the
object of unrequited desire. Now, Angel (whom I now saw
coming toward me out of the set of swinging wooden doors
to the left of the reception desk) must have encountered
panting men from adolescence onward. I would have to ask
her how it made her feel. Right now she looked washed
out, and her stride did not have its usual assurance.

'Are you okay?' I asked anxiously.

She nodded, but not as if she meant it. 'I'm just going to

go home and lie down,' she said. 'I don't think I've ever been this tired in my life. And I'm hungry. Really, really hungry.'

'Need help?'

'Nah. Shelby'll be home in an hour.' She hadn't spoken to Arthur directly, but her next words were aimed at him. 'If you're not home by then, I'll call Bubba.'

Bubba Sewell was my lawyer.

'See you later,' I said, and she was out the glass doors and into the parking lot. I watched her reach her car, unlock it, stretch her arms up and rotate her shoulders to relax, each movement economical and controlled despite her weariness.

'Come this way, Roe,' Arthur said, snapping me back to the unwelcome present. He was holding open the wooden doors, nodding at the woman in uniform on duty at the desk behind bullet-proof glass, gesturing me forward. As I went through the doors, he put his hand on my back to steer me, a controlling gesture I particularly dislike. I don't much care for being touched casually. I stiffened a little, but put up with it.

When I realized I was only tolerating his touching me because he had once been my lover, I stepped away a little quicker, leaving his hand behind, and his arm dropped to his side.

Arthur waved a hand at his own little cubicle to usher me in. He indicated the only other chair besides the one behind the desk, and murmured something about being back in a minute. Then he vanished, leaving me nothing to do but examine his 'office'. It was a bit like being at a car dealership where each salesman has to usher you into a little area partitioned off at neck level, and there present you with pages of scrawled figures. I could tell Arthur worked there; there was a picture of little Lorna, though none of Lynn. But there wasn't clutter, there wasn't even much office material on the desk: no Rolodex, no blotter, no stapler. There were stacked in and out trays, and a chipped Christmas coffee mug holding some pens and pencils. That was it. I'd exhausted the possibilities of Arthur's office.

Then I observed that though the partition walls were made of beige metal and padded with what looked like carpet, each panel contained a Plexiglas window. I could see down the row of similar cubicles. Lynn was two squares away, bent over some paperwork on her desk. She looked up as I was still gazing curiously in her direction. She gave me an unreadable stare and then looked down at her desk pointedly.

From being mildly uneasy at being here, I escalated instantly into very uncomfortable. Had I been brought here as some ploy in Lynn and Arthur's marital wars?

Arthur reappeared just as I was thinking of leaving. He was holding two unmatched mugs of coffee, one with cream and sugar and one black. He put the black in front of me. 'I remembered that was the way you like it,' he said.

I could read nothing in his tone. I thanked him and tried a sip. It was awful. I put it down carefully.

'Why am I here, Arthur?'

'Because you had a very public quarrel with Beverly Rillington yesterday. Because she was attacked and her purse stolen last night. When I heard Mrs Youngblood had been present during the quarrel, I called her in too. Faron Henske just finished questioning her.'

80

So that's why a robbery detective was handling the case. They were treating the attack on Beverly as a robbery gone berserk. 'Why couldn't you just ask me about it at my house, or over the phone, or at the library?'

'Because this was the best place,' he said, very male tough policeman.

I raised my eyebrows slightly. I pushed my gold glasses back up on my nose. 'Then ask your questions.'

So we went through the miserable scene at the library again: the rising rage of Beverly, the arrival of Angel, Angel's exchange with Beverly, the gradual defusing of the crisis.

'Did you think Beverly was physically threatening you?' Arthur asked quietly. He was sitting back in his chair, his gaze locked on me in a way I'd once considered flattering and exciting.

'I had a second of worry.'

'Weren't you glad your bodyguard was there to handle it for you?'

I could feel my eyes fly open even wider, my shoulders stiffen.

Arthur looked pleased to get such a response. 'Did you think we wouldn't figure it out, Roe? Back when the Julius family turned up, we checked out your friends the Young-bloods. Shelby Youngblood and your husband have quite a history together, don't they?'

'Martin and Shelby have been friends since Vietnam.'

'Involved in some murky doings after that, weren't they?'

'What are you getting at, Arthur? You know Martin was out of town last night. Are you implying that one of the Youngbloods attacked Beverly Rillington because she gave me a few bad moments in the library?'

'There are telephones in Chicago.' Arthur had been leaning negligently back in his chair. Now he abandoned the relaxed pose and leaned forward, his hard eyes still fixed on me.

'So you're saying that my husband was so upset that I had a few words with Beverly – in front of many witnesses – that he told the Youngbloods to beat her up.'

'I didn't say that. But it seems pretty coincidental that after a decade of giving people grief, Beverly Rillington gets beaten within an inch of her life just after a quarrel with you and your bodyguard.' He gave the last two words a twist that was distinctly unpleasant. I began to think that Arthur had gone off the deep end of the pool without checking to see if there was any water.

'You're certainly not suggesting that I did it,' I said reasonably, though I felt anything but reasonable. 'I think Beverly has a few inches and pounds on me.'

'No,' Arthur said, never letting up on the stare. 'No, not you. But someone who cares for you.'

I started to say, 'What about someone who cares for Angel?' Because it seemed to me that Angel had been insulted publicly too, and if the theory that the incident in the library had sparked this attack held any water, Angel could be the inspiration for the beating far more feasibly than I. No one ever forgot Angel.

But expressing this would be tantamount to pointing the finger at Shelby, at least in Arthur's present state of mind.

'So. You're sure I didn't hurt Beverly. So – why am I sitting here being questioned if you are telling me you're sure I didn't do it?'

And without pausing to give him a chance to respond,

I gathered up my purse and stalked out of Spacolec. My back was tense with expecting him to call me at any moment, but he didn't.

Like most of my grand gestures, this one was ruined by the situation I came upon out in the parking lot. Instead of sliding into my car and speeding away with a spray of gravel, I had to deal with two more angry people.

Angel was standing in front of her car, her face expressionless but her attitude tense. Beside her, talking into a radio, was Detective Paul Allison, who for once looked agitated. On the hood of Angel's car, giving the impression of a spilled bag of garbage, was a battered black imitation-leather purse, gap-mouthed and leaking the miscellany of a woman's life: comb, wallet, Kleenex, crumpled shopping lists, a tube of mints.

I recognized it. It was Beverly's purse, surely the purse that had been stolen from her during the attack the night before.

Chapter Six

'Is this your car?' Paul Allison said sharply, hanging up the radio in its place in his vehicle, a tan Ford, pulled in next to Angel's.

It took me a moment to realize that Paul was speaking to me.

'No,' I said. 'Mine's this one.' I pointed.

I'd known Paul, at least to speak to, for years, and he'd never changed; he was about five ten, slim, with light blue eyes and thin light hair, worn cut short on the sides and combed straight back. Paul was in his midforties. He had a sharp nose and a square jaw, thin lips and a pale complexion. If you were a civilian, you had to know Paul for a while for him even to register; he was that nondescript in appearance.

But from the time I'd dated Arthur, I knew Paul was unpopular among his fellow officers who saw Paul as being secretive, self-righteous, and charmless. Paul didn't drink or smoke, and barely had tolerance for those who did; he didn't hunt, or watch football, or even buy nudie magazines. His brief marriage to Sally had been his only one. Apparently, law enforcement was Paul's life, as it had been for his former boss, Jack Burns.

'I told you it was my car,' Angel said with barely maintained patience.

Since I was keeping a sharp eye on Paul, I could see rage roll over his face like a tidal wave. He was so angry I was surprised to see there wasn't a gun in his hand, that he wasn't ordering Angel down on the ground.

'Paul!' I said sharply.

He blinked and looked at me. I put myself right by Angel. His eyes went from Angel down to me, back up to Angel, with the strangest expression.

Being weighed and found wanting was never a pleasant experience, even being found wanting by someone you didn't give a flip for. I sighed before I said, 'Could you explain why this purse is here?' It seemed safe to talk now; Paul's face had resumed its normal color and his eyes were focused and sane again.

'I was just about to ask this woman the same thing,' Paul said, in a much calmer voice.

'I'm Angel Youngblood,' she said, in an equally cool way. 'I found this purse on the hood of my car when I came to get in after coming out of the Law Enforcement Complex, and then the convenience store.' She nodded her head toward the Shop-So-Kwik about thirty feet from the end of the Spacolec parking lot. She had a little bag in her right hand. She waved it.

Paul made a gesture, and in response, Angel opened the bag. Inside was a little package of Tostitos, a Diet Coke, and a giant cookie in its own cellophane wrapper. 'Hungry,' she said by way of explanation.

I had *never* seen Angel eat food like this; tasty junk, but junk.

'So the purse was exactly like this when you returned?'

Paul asked. His voice resumed its normal flat, faintly sour tone.

'No, I opened it and poked in it to try to see who it belonged to,' Angel said with perfect logic. 'I looked around the parking lot first to see if I could spot a woman who might have put it here, but when I didn't see anyone, I looked inside. I was just about to open the snap on the wallet when you popped out of your car.'

Paul pulled a pencil out of his shirt pocket, turned the purse over on the hood of the car, and levered out the wallet. He stuck in the end of the pencil to work the snap, and unfolded the wallet with it. It fell open to a driver's license. The picture and the name were that of Beverly Rillington.

I wasn't surprised, since I'd been sure I recognized the purse. But Angel drew in a sharp breath, the equivalent of a scream for those of us who don't count on danger as a way of life.

'Maybe we'd better go in and talk,' Paul said, and I didn't think he was making a suggestion.

'No.' My mother would be arriving with troops if I didn't get home and call her, and there was no sense in making more of this than necessary.

'What?' Paul had a puzzled expression, as if he hadn't quite understood what I meant by 'No.'

'When I drove into the parking lot and stopped by Angel's car, the purse wasn't there. When Angel went by my car, the purse wasn't *there*. And what a senseless thing for either of us to do, put Beverly's purse out. We might as well go on and put the handcuffs on ourselves! Gee, here we are at the Law Enforcement Complex, let's put incriminating evidence on the hood of a car?'

Paul's thin mouth curved in a reluctant smile. It was the first time I'd had a glimpse of what Sally had seen in him.

'Okay, Roe. But if you didn't leave the purse on Mrs Youngblood's car, and Mrs Youngblood didn't, who did? Why?'

Angel looked down at me, and I knew our blank gazes were a match. But Angel could see when a thought reached my brain, and shook her head, a tiny gesture as firm as a hand clapped over my mouth.

'We're not detectives,' I said, looking at Paul. Angel unwrapped the cookie from the bag and started to eat it. Since her mouth was full, she had to shrug.

Though Paul fussed at us some more, he eventually hooked a pencil under the purse strap and carried it into Spacolec. Angel had finished the cookie and opened the Tostitos and the Coke.

'Someone has it in for you,' I observed.

'How do you figure that?' Angel asked around a Tostito.

'The flowers, sent to get you in trouble with your husband. The ribbon around the cat's neck, to let you know you weren't secure. The beating of Beverly Rillington after you had a standoff with her in the library. The placing of the purse on your car.'

'That's the oddest thing,' Angel said. She gave me a look full of significance. And I couldn't read it.

'Hell, it's all odd!' I said, puzzled. 'But you mean, because putting the purse out here was so open? Everything else could be done in the dark or long distance, so to speak.'

Angel looked away and finally nodded.

I had to restrain myself from asking her to explain all this Enigmatic she was giving me. We'd known each other for two years now, been neighbors for that time, and I thought we were as close friends as we could be, given the fact that she was my employee and we had very different characters. I did at least know Angel well enough to be sure that she would tell me what she was thinking when she was good and ready, and not a moment before.

By the look she was giving me, I could tell Angel thought I was being as dense as I thought she was being secretive. Mutually baffled and exasperated, we got in our respective cars and went home, Angel obeying the speed limit meticulously all the way. I followed behind her, driving automatically. My state of mind might best be described as confused.

I couldn't help but remember Arthur's long absence, his return with the coffee. Had Arthur Smith planted that purse on the hood of Angel's car while she was in the market? If he thought discrediting Angel and perhaps by extension her husband and mine would somehow induce me to think more kindly of him, Arthur was not just mistaken, but seriously deranged.

I trailed slowly into the house, just in time to hear the phone ring. I dashed down the hall, past the stairs, to the second door on the right leading to our study/library/ television room.

'What now?' my mother asked in her cool voice. But I could hear the mixture of anxiety and exasperation underlying it, the two emotions that seemed to dominate in her dealings with me.

I glanced at the desk clock; of course, it was four on the dot.

'It's okay. I just got in from Spacolec.'

'I think it's outrageous, them asking you to come in to that place. They should have driven out to your home or talked to you in that new wing you gave the library.'

'Mother!' No one was supposed to know I'd given the kickoff donation for the new staff area. 'How'd you find out?'

'I have my ways,' she said calmly, without a trace of humor.

'Well, don't you ever tell anyone else,' I said hotly. If my gift became common knowledge, it would be pretty hard for me to keep working at the library; that wasn't logical, but it was true.

'Did that woman really get hurt badly, Aurora?' My mother was back on track, even if I wasn't.

'Sam told me that she might die.'

'What a terrible thing. And since you had an argument with her the same day, I know what you must be feeling.'

She did, too. It was a milder version of having a fight with your spouse, who subsequently drives off and has a car wreck. That had happened when Mother was still with my father, when I was twelve. He'd left soon after, neck brace and all.

We talked about Beverly Rillington for a little longer, and then my mother asked me which policeman I'd talked to today.

I'd been dreading that question. 'Arthur,' I told her reluctantly.

I swear, I could hear the phone line sizzle. My mother has

never forgiven Arthur for dating me and then dumping me to marry Lynn Liggett, who was visibly pregnant at the wedding. (Well, it certainly hadn't been my favorite episode in the Life of Roe either, but I'd weathered it and eventually let it go.) God bless my mother, in some respects she was totally motherlike; anyone who made me suffer was in her black book forever.

'Roe, you stay away from that man,' she said, in her Absolute Last Word voice. 'He has separated from his wife. Last week Patty showed him a townhouse over where you used to live, and he was moving in by himself. You don't want to look as if you're paying him any attention whatsoever.'

'I hope they work it out and get back together,' I said fervently. My suspicion that Arthur had called me in to the station to wave me in Lynn's face was correct. I'd gotten over my initial rush of anger, and now felt simply appalled that Arthur would do something so low. I'd never seen that side of him, and I didn't want to believe it had always been there.

As I microwaved a low-fat dinner I'd gotten at the grocery for just such an evening, I realized I wasn't exactly looking forward to Martin's nightly call. It was going to be hard to explain some of the things that had happened to me today, and harder still (actually impossible) to explain them in a way that didn't make him angry at someone. And it would be futile anger, since he was too far away to act on it. Also, I didn't want the peculiar incident of the ribbon on Madeleine's neck to cause him concern.

But I don't like to lie, and I'm not good at it.

Luckily for me, it was late when he called. He'd gone

out to dinner with some other executives, and they'd made an evening of it. Martin is not much of a drinker, since he despises people who lose their control; but I could tell he'd had up to his limit. So he was sleepy and sentimental over the phone, and it was easy to tell him that I'd give him a rundown on the day's happenings when he came home.

That night I tossed and turned, suffering an unusual episode of sleeplessness.

I couldn't track down the source of the anxiety that was keeping me awake.

The security system was on, so I knew no one could break in; but it was gusty and raining outside, and I could hear the wind moaning around the corner of the house. I would doze off, only to jerk awake with the feeling of having just missed something vital, something to which I should have been paying close attention.

Every time I woke up, I thought of something new to worry over, either Angel's pregnancy and its effect on her marriage, or the bizarre episodes of the ribbon and the purse, or the sight of Jack Burns falling, falling . . . and Angel and Shelby would need a bigger place, they could never live in that glorified one-room apartment with a baby . . .

I got up to go to the bathroom, I went downstairs to get a drink of water, I worked a crossword puzzle, I finished the book I'd started in Dr Zelman's office.

At four-thirty, I gave up. I wrapped myself in the dark blue robe Mother had given me for Christmas, slid into my slippers, and went downstairs, officially up for the day. The coffeepot's automatic timer hadn't had a chance to kick in; I switched it to On and heard the comforting hiss of the water starting through the brewing cycle.

Perhaps the paper had come? Morning coffee just didn't seem right without a newspaper. It was awfully early; I realized I really had no idea how early the Atlanta paper and the Lawrenceton paper landed in our driveway.

Tying the belt of my robe more securely around me, I stepped out onto the front porch. The rain was still coming down lightly, giving the air a sharp cool edge. I reached inside the door for an umbrella and unwisely opened it before I pushed out the screen door. Of course it got wedged in the doorway and I had to do an inordinate amount of pushing, angling, and cursing to get it through.

Going outside at such a strange hour in the mild cool rain was a little adventure. I needed a flashlight, too, but the umbrella incident had made me so grumpy I refused to be sensible. There was a huge strong automatic light in our backyard, but not one in the front; outside the range of the porch light the driveway was in darkness. I followed the stepping-stones leading to the right so I could walk down the driveway. We'd had it paved the year before: at least I wasn't stumbling over gravel, but the asphalt was streaming with rain, and my slippers were getting soaked.

I went to the area where the Atlanta paper usually landed, and sure enough, there it was in a plastic sleeve. Feeling that virtue had been rewarded, I tucked it under my umbrella-holding arm and lifted the skirt of my bathrobe with the other. I turned to go back inside, happily confident that the coffee would be ready and that I had cinnamon rolls in the freezer I could pop into the microwave. The Lawrenceton paper would just have to wait until light.

I was concentrating on watching my feet as I transferred from the driveway to the stepping-stones, but something butted on the edge of my awareness. The light had been behind me as I left the house, but now that I was returning, I could see a few things I hadn't noticed before; and one of the things I could make out was a bush planted where no bush had been the day before.

I paused on the seventh stepping-stone from the front porch. I tilted my head and stared, trying to puzzle out what I was seeing. A large dark heap, right in front of the foundation plantings . . . my slippers would get thoroughly soaked if I left the stepping-stones to investigate. I shifted my feet, peering with no better luck at the vague and immobile shape, and realized that my slippers were doomed.

I stepped gingerly onto the soggy grass, clutching the paper and umbrella.

Seconds later I'd dropped both.

The dark shape on my lawn was Shelby Youngblood. He was unconscious, lying on his side, wearing a dark raincoat with a hood. He was immobile because someone had hit him on the back of his head. When I pulled the hood away from his face, the hood was filled with blood.

I foolishly wasted seconds trying to arrange my umbrella to shelter the wound. Finally realizing I was acting like a woman with no sense, I tore into the house and hit 911 on the phone in the study. Once I'd explained to the calm voice on the other end what my problem was and where I was, I hung up and punched in Angel's number. For some reason, I feared she was hurt too. But she answered, in the groggy normal voice of someone wakened at four forty-five by the telephone ringing.

'Come outside, now,' I gabbled. 'Shelby's hurt, but I've already called the ambulance.' My eardrum echoed with the sound of her receiver crashing down. I slammed down my own telephone and ran back outside, my heart and lungs in a race to see which could work fastest. But I had pulled open the right-hand drawer on Martin's desk as I dialed Angel, and this time there was a flashlight in my hand.

I crouched by Shelby in the rain, which of course picked this moment to come down in torrents. Though anyone lit up by a flashlight in the dark is not going to look great, it seemed to me that Shelby was an especially bad color. I held the umbrella over him, wondering if there was anything I could do.

Well, I should see if he was still alive.

I slid my hand inside his raincoat, found that Shelby didn't have a shirt on, and lay my hand on his chest. It was moving in and out, how deeply I couldn't gauge; but Shelby was breathing, and at the moment that was all I cared about.

I'd been concentrating on him so hard that I didn't hear Angel coming. Suddenly she was crouching on the other side of her husband. She was barefoot and in a nightgown, with a shirt of Shelby's pulled over her. Her hair hung in a loose tangle around her narrow face.

'Is he breathing?' Her voice was sharp.

'Yes.'

'You called 911?'

'Yes.'

'How long ago?'

'Five minutes,' I guessed. 'They're on this side of town, they'll be here any minute.'

Sure enough, I saw the blinking red lights far down the road toward town. I tried to pray, but the rain was plastering my hair to my skull and dripping down my neck, and Shelby seemed so close to leaving us that all I could do was urge the ambulance forward mentally, hoping that the best team Lawrenceton had to offer was on duty this cool spring night.

I had a flash of sense as the young man and woman were loading Shelby into the back of the ambulance. I dashed into the house, opened the coat closet, and yanked out Martin's lined raincoat. Pounding down the porch steps, I yelled to Angel just as she was about to climb in the ambulance. I could see the flash of annoyance on her face, but she realized she needed more body coverage than she had, and she turned her back to me and held her arms a little out and down, and I slid the coat over her wet arms and nightgown as quickly as I could.

With a scream of the siren the ambulance was off, and I could finally go inside. Everything I had on was soaked through, and though the morning was not really cold, I was chilled to the bone. I stripped right inside the front door so I wouldn't get more water on my wooden floors than I absolutely had to – I could see the splotches left from my previous entrances and exits – and I sprinted upstairs to the shower to let the hot water wash the dirt and rain off. I dressed in record time, turning on the heat lamp in the bathroom to start my hair drying, and I plugged in my usual handheld dryer too; but with a mass of thick hair like mine, it took too long, and I drove to the hospital with damp hair that was curling and waving around my face like streamers of confetti.

I'd taken the time to use my emergency key to the Youngbloods' apartment to grab some clothes for Angel. It felt very strange to be poking through her things, dropping the basic garments into a plastic Wal-Mart bag. I included shoes, a toothbrush, and a hairbrush at the last second.

Angel was sitting in the emergency waiting room at the little Lawrenceton Hospital, her hands folded and her face blank. She didn't recognize me for a moment.

'What have they told you?' I asked.

'Ahhh . . . he's got a concussion, a bad one. He has to stay here for a few days.' Her voice was expressionless, numb.

'He's going to be all right?'

'We'll see when he wakes up.'

'Listen, then, Angel . . . are you hearing me?'

'Yes. I hear you.' She was a pathetic sight. She was as wet as I had been, and she had pulled on Martin's raincoat over her wet clothes, so she was warm enough for the moment; but the damp was sealed inside the coat. Her blond hair hung in rattails down her back, and her feet were bare and streaked with dirt and bits of grass. The passivity of her strong body was so upsetting I had to retreat into briskness.

'I brought some clothes and shoes, and your toothbrush, and your hairbrush. Is Shelby in a room yet?'

'No, he's still in emergency. They brought in a portable X-ray machine, and since I'm pregnant I had to leave. They didn't even want me to put on the heavy apron, they wanted me out.'

'Well. We're going to find out what room they're going to put him in, and you're going to go in there and take a shower, and by then the cafeteria here will be open, and we're going to go in there and eat.'

Angel blinked. She seemed a little more aware.

'That sounds okay,' she said hesitantly. 'But no one will be with him.'

'You don't need to watch him, they're doing it for you. He's going to be okay,' I said soothingly. 'Now, I'm going to find the admissions person, and see about getting all this started.'

The 'admissions person' was glad to see me, since she hadn't been able to get much out of Angel besides Shelby's name and his birthday. I gave the clerk Shelby's insurance program group number, the same as Martin's since they were both covered by Pan-Am Agra's group plan. I gave the clerk an address, next of kin, everything but Social Security number, and I promised her Angel would remember that after breakfast. By dint of being cheerful and persistent, I was able to get Shelby's future room number, and took Angel there, resisting the impulse to ask to see Shelby myself.

After fifteen minutes with Shelby's admissions hygiene kit, a hot shower, and clean clothes, Angel was a new woman, and after we talked our way into the employee cafeteria and she downed a plate of grits and sausage and toast, she was approaching normality.

It was while we were sitting there, Angel with another glass of orange juice and me with my third cup of coffee, that the deputy found us.

He was a young man I didn't know, dressed in a crisp uniform. He seemed concerned and wary, all at the same time. He introduced himself as Jimmy Henske.

'Do you have a relative on the town force?' I asked.

'Yes, ma'am, my uncle Faron. You know Uncle Faron?'

'Yes, I do.' He'd questioned Angel the day before, Arthur had told me. Faron was a good ole boy, with a heavy Southern drawl and an unreconstructed attitude about women on the force and black people having power and money. But Faron was also a courteous and anxious man who had no idea he was biased and would swear on a stack of family Bibles that he was fair to one and all.

Jimmy had the family coloring and build. The Henskes tended to be tall, thin, and reddish, with high-bridged noses and big hands and feet (including the women). Jimmy was trying to pay courteous attention to his conversation with me, but his eyes kept straying to Angel. I sighed, trying to keep it quiet.

'Now, Ms Teagarden, I understand you found Mr Young-blood in your yard?' He'd torn his gaze away from her to begin his questioning.

I told him what had happened, said I hadn't heard any noises in the night (though with the wind and rain it would have been surprising if I had), and explained that my husband was out of town. Jimmy Henske instantly came to attention; if he'd been a bird dog, he would've been pointing his nose. Clearly, he was wondering if Angel had bashed her husband because Shelby was sneaking over to see me. Or perhaps (and his gaze swung my way) I'd done it when he'd tried to make advances to me?

I did my best to disabuse him of those suspicions by telling him that while Martin was gone, Shelby sometimes patrolled the yard, and that I was sure he must have been doing so the night before because of the incident of Madeleine's ribbon.

It was lucky Shelby had taken Madeleine in to Dr Jamerson, I thought as I explained the incident to Deputy Henske, because it was confirmation that we suspected someone had been on my property.

Jimmy didn't know what to make of a prowler sneaking into the yard to tie a ribbon on Madeleine's neck, and to tell the truth, I didn't either; but I was glad to think the solution was his problem rather than mine.

After a confused-looking Jimmy Henske left for Spacolec, his little notebook full of indecipherable squiggles, a nurse came to tell us Shelby was in his room, and conscious.

Angel was on her feet faster than lightning, and I put our trays on the appropriate rack and followed at a slower pace. She needed time alone with Shelby, and I had to call Pan-Am Agra and tell Martin's production head that he would be short a crew leader that day, and for several days following. I took care of that little chore, wondered if I should pick up Shelby's paycheck, and snapped to when an orderly eyed me curiously. I was standing by the pay telephone in the hall, my hand still resting on the receiver, staring blankly at the coin input slot. Lack of sleep was catching up with me as the emergency-produced adrenaline ebbed.

A glance at my watch told me it was all of eight o'clock by then.

It had already been a long day.

With a sinking heart, I realized I had to go in to work. With Beverly in the hospital, it was especially important for me to show up. I wondered how she was doing. Well, I was in the place to find out.

I went to the nurses' station and inquired about both Beverly and her mother, Selena. The nurse, a young woman I'd never seen before, told me briefly that both mother and daughter had died in the course of the night.

I sat in the waiting area for a while with a magazine on my lap, hoping no one would talk to me, feeling sick at heart.

When my mind finally began functioning again, I was almost sorry. My thoughts were all unpleasant ones. Could it really be a coincidence that Beverly Rillington, who had threatened Angel publicly, and Angel's husband Shelby had both been admitted to the hospital with head wounds in the same week?

Finally I roused myself to find Shelby's room, and knocked gently on the door. Angel stuck her head out.

'How is he?' I whispered.

'Come in.'

Shelby looked horrible. He was asleep, but Angel told me in a low voice that the doctor had said he must not sleep long at a stretch. He had to be woken up periodically. There was a good reason for this, but my overloaded system didn't absorb it.

'He didn't see whoever did it, Roe, he doesn't remember anything since he ate supper last night. He didn't remember putting on his clothes and his raincoat, or why he thought he ought to go outside . . .'

I stared at Shelby while Angel murmured on and on. She was chatty with relief now that she was reasonably sure Shelby was going to recover.

Shelby's face was stubbly with unshaven beard, a state I'd seen before, but the skin underneath the bristles was a distressing gray. The hair protruding from underneath the bandage was matted with blood and stringy from drying with rainwater on it. There was a huge dark bruise on his right arm, which Angel thought was a defense wound. Shelby had taken a blow on that arm defending his own head, but it hadn't worked a second time. One of his ribs was broken, too, Angel said . . . he'd been kicked when he was down.

I didn't have to look at Angel to know she would kill whoever had done this to Shelby if she could find him.

After a while, Angel ran down. She stood looking at Shelby as if her eyes could glue him to her, as if his life could not escape him if she were there to make sure it stayed.

I was thinking my own thoughts. Why hadn't Shelby heard the attack coming? He'd made his living as a body-guard for years. He was tough and quick and ruthless. Had the sound of the rain and wind dulled Shelby's senses, so the approach of the trespasser was totally unexpected?

Or had he turned to see someone he knew, someone he did not think of as an enemy?

Chapter Seven

Normally, when Martin returned from a business trip I got to tell him about the kid who threw up on the Berenstain Bears book, or what the plumber had told me when he'd come to repair the hot water heater.

When he walked in the front door late that afternoon, I hardly knew where to begin. As it turned out, Martin had stopped at the Pan-Am Agra plant, so he already knew that Shelby was in the hospital. After his first anxious questions, he settled down to listen with that total concentration that made him such a good executive.

I think Martin was just as shocked by Angel's pregnancy as by Shelby being attacked in our front yard. And when I told him about the ribbon around Madeleine's neck and the deaths of Beverly and Selena Rillington, he had to get up and walk around the kitchen.

It was still raining, and I watched the drops hit the large window by the table where Martin and I usually ate, the window overlooking the side of the garage and the steps up to the apartment, as well as some lovely pink azaleas hidden now by the darkness. The drops might hit at random, but they ran down the glass with monotonous regularity. The rain increased my sense of being stockaded against the danger outside, besieged.

Martin strode through the dining room, out into the

living room, back through the archway into the dining room. He circled the table and shot back into the kitchen again, stopping by the window to stare out into the blackness.

'Who sent the flowers?' he asked abruptly, and I glanced into the dining room to see that they were still in their vase on the table. A few blossoms were shriveling, and one or two bits of baby's breath had fallen to the polished surface of the old table.

The delivery of the flowers seemed so long ago I'd forgotten about it completely. Now, when I added it to my list of happenings, Martin gave me a sharp look, one that said effectively, 'All this you didn't tell me over the telephone?'

Martin often reminded me of the Roman officer in the New Testament, the one who told Jesus that when he said 'Go,' people went, and when he said 'Come,' people hopped to it. Now, he was apparently trying to decide what he could do about this situation, and he was angrily seeing that there was nothing he could do.

'Do you think the little hospital here is the best place for Shelby, can he get the best care available? I could have him moved to Atlanta by ambulance.' Martin looked almost happy at this prospect of action.

'I don't believe there's any need of that,' I said gently. 'Besides, the doctors here are very aware that the city hospitals have things the Lawrenceton Hospital doesn't have, and they would have sent him to the city without hesitation if they thought his situation warranted that. Plus, you know,' I said even more gently, 'that's Angel's call, not yours.'

Diverted back to Angel's pregnancy, Martin said what I'd been dreading he'd say.

'I like Angel just as much as you, but don't you think it's stretching belief to have her turn up pregnant when Shelby's had a vasectomy? She worked out with Jack Burns and she's going to his funeral, but she blasted him in public when he gave her a ticket. And she didn't react at all when they turned him over the other day. I don't want to believe anything bad about Angel, but doesn't that all add up?'

'You know, Shelby asked me if I'd seen anyone else out here when he was gone,' I said evenly.

'What'd you tell him?' Martin turned to me, hands thrust in his pockets to keep them still.

'I slapped the tar out of him.' I looked at Martin steadily, blocking my faintly guilty memory of Shelby's embrace from my mind, so he couldn't read it in my face.

Martin looked back at me, eyebrows up in surprise.

'And – what did he do?' Martin asked faintly.

'He believed that he is the father of Angel's child.'

Martin slowly took a deep breath, released it, smiled. 'Okay. So is he going to get rechecked?'

'He'll have to if they don't want any more children,' I said.

'I can't believe old Shelby is going to be a father,' Martin said absently, shaking his head.

I bit my lip and looked down so Martin wouldn't see the tears well into my eyes. He pulled his reading glasses (a recent necessity) out of his shirt pocket suddenly, and went to the wall phone to flip through the tiny Lawrenceton directory.

He punched in numbers and stood waiting, his face in its

executive mode: mouth in straight hard line, sharp eyes, impatient stance. I thought it was pretty sexy, providing he dropped the look when he turned to me.

'The room number?' he asked me crisply. I gave it to him, propped my chin on my hand, and watched my husband as he talked to Angel, and then said a few words to Shelby.

'He's still groggy,' Martin informed me when he had hung up the phone. 'But better. Angel said they want to keep him one more day for observation, then he can come home, providing he stays away from work for a few days.' Martin clearly felt better since he'd done something, even if it was only punch numbers on a phone.

I glanced down at my watch, and saw to my surprise that it was nearly eleven o'clock. I'd been up almost the whole night the night before, and gone through a great deal of excitement and anxiety since then. Martin's homecoming had given me a jolt of energy, but suddenly I felt as if I'd run into a wall.

'I have to go up to bed,' I said, and heard the weariness in my voice.

'Of course, honey,' Martin said instantly. 'You haven't had any sleep.' He put his heavy arm around me and we started up the stairs. 'I'll give you your present in the morning,' he murmured.

'Okay.'

'You *are* tired.'

'Won't be this tired in the morning,' I mumbled, I hoped in a promising way. 'I am glad you're home.'

I pulled off the clothes I'd pulled on so hastily so many hours ago and gratefully slipped into a nightgown, realizing that I had no memory of work that day at all, though I'd gone in and (I supposed) functioned more or less normally. I brushed my teeth and washed my face because I am constitutionally unable to go to bed without that little routine, and I was vaguely aware of Martin unpacking as I sank into sleep.

Before I open my eyes in the morning, I try to remember what day it is. There's always that happy moment when it's finally Saturday, and I don't have to go anywhere I don't want to. I think that's one of the reasons I had wanted to go back to work; otherwise every day was Saturday, and that little happiness was gone.

I opened one eye and looked at my bedside clock. It read nine-twenty. Since that was clearly impossible, I closed the eye again and snuggled into my pillow. But the room certainly seemed light, and I could feel the emptiness of the other side of the bed. Reluctantly, I opened both eyes and wriggled closer to the clock. It was still nine-twenty.

I hadn't slept that late in years.

For ten minutes or so, I basked in the novelty of being still in bed at such a late hour. I was too awake to drift back to sleep. From the lack of movement downstairs, I thought Martin was gone. He often went in to work for a few hours on weekends, especially when he'd been out of town; or maybe he'd gone to the Athletic Club to play some racquetball. Going downstairs in a nightgown this late seemed faintly sleazy, so I took my shower first and pulled on my favorite Saturday jeans and a green T-shirt. To atone for my laziness, I carried down a hamper of dirty clothes and started a load of wash before I even poured my coffee. Martin had made a full pot and left it on for me, with a clean cup waiting invitingly beside the pot. He'd also left, squarely in the middle of the table by the window, a package wrapped in white paper and topped with a blue bow.

I drank my first cup of coffee and read the Lawrenceton paper to postpone the pleasure of opening the package. And the paper dampened my happiness some; the attack on Shelby had made the front page, which was not too surprising. But what was surprising was that the incident of the bow on the cat and the body of Jack Burns landing in the yard were included in the story, tying all the different incidents together in a way that left me disturbed.

I'd been sure Jack Burns had been killed because he knew the identity of a local who was being hidden in Lawrenceton under the Witness Protection Program. I couldn't see what that had to do with Angel's unknown admirer. Combining all these incidents, the story implied my house was radiating evil, as though it was an eminently suitable candidate for exorcism. I wasn't surprised to see a stranger's name on the byline: Sally wouldn't have written it that way.

I tried to regain my relaxed mood by reading the Garden Club meeting report, which was usually a hoot. It didn't fail me today. My old friend Mrs Lyndower (Neecy) Dawson had wreaked havoc by proposing that the war memorial outside the courthouse be surrounded by ivy instead of having its planting regularly switched by the club. Reading between the Garden Club correspondent's careful lines, one could surmise that the ensuing debate had created bad blood that might last as much as a year, by which time Neecy could have forgotten she'd made the proposal. Or have gone to her great reward in the Garden in the Sky, as the Garden Club membership might have put it.

A flash of white and orange outside caught my attention, and I saw that Madeleine, to whom I'd given scant attention the past two days, had finally been driven to desperate measures. She was stalking a sparrow foraging in the grass. One thing I admired about cats was their focus; I'd never had a pet as I was growing up, so observing Madeleine had been an education for me (one I sometimes felt I could have done without).

However, when Madeleine bothered to hunt, the process was impressive – the intensity of her concentration, the stealth of her approach, the narrowness of her vision. *Can birds see color?* I wondered.

Whether it was Madeleine's marmalade stripes or her bulk that attracted the bird's attention, this sparrow took off. Madeleine sat up and directed a baleful gaze after the bird, and began to clean her paws in a sulky way. I was recalled to my obligations, and fed her; she did her very best running when she heard me call her for food.

Then I had the pleasure of opening my package. It was heavy, and I wondered how Martin had managed to cope with it on the flight home. I slid off the ribbon and put it aside, and tore off the paper. The box was a plain brown one of thick cardboard, not one of the thin ones that clothes come in.

Not jewelry, not clothes . . . hmmmm.

Books. Seven books by some of my favorite mystery writers. Bookmarks from a Chicago bookstore protruded from each one, and I opened the top book, a Sharyn Mc-Crumb, at the marked page.

Each one was signed. Not only signed, but personalized.

I examined each book happily, looking forward to hours

of reading, and tried to think of a special place to keep my gift.

While I was still smiling, the phone rang.

There was silence on the other end of the line after I answered. It wasn't empty silence, like when the other person has realized he didn't mean to call your number after all and has hung up – this was heavy silence, breathing silence. My smile slid off my face and I could feel my scalp crawl.

'Hello?' I said again, hoping against hope someone would speak.

Someone did.

'Are you alone?' asked a man's voice. And the phone went dead.

I tried to slow my breathing, reminded myself that everyone gets prank or obscene calls from time to time (such is humankind's determination to communicate, on whatever low plane) and I should not particularly be upset by this. But I felt so alone today; Martin wasn't here, and the garage apartment was empty, too.

The phone rang again, and I jumped. I stared at it, wondering whether to answer it or not. As it kept ringing, I crossed the hall to the study and waited for the answering machine to come on. Martin had recorded the message, and hearing his voice made me feel better. When the recording ended and the signal beep came, the voice leaving the message was also reassuring.

'Sally!' I stopped the recording and picked up the phone. 'What are you up to?'

'I wondered if you were free to take a little ride with me,'

Sally said. 'I didn't know if that husband of yours was in town or not.'

'He's in town, but not at home right now, so I'm foot-loose,' I said, relieved at having a reason to leave the house without calling it retreating in fear. 'Where are you going to go?'

'I'm going to drive to that airport where Jack Burns was taking flying lessons, the one where he rented the plane before he took his *final* flying lesson, so to speak. I need an extra person – I have a plan – and since I haven't gotten to talk to you in a coon's age, I thought I'd combine the two goals.'

Put like that, how could I resist?

'Want me to drive in and meet you at the newspaper office?'

'That's where I am now. That'd be great.'

'Okay. Give me a few minutes, I'll be on my way.'

I called the hospital to ask Angel if she needed anything urgently, and she told me that Shelby was much better, but still didn't remember anything about the attack. She sounded a lot better herself. She'd run home the night before to change clothes, and she told me she might come home to take a nap in the afternoon if he continued to improve.

Then I called Martin. If he was at the plant, he wasn't answering his phone. I left a message at the Athletic Club with the intimidatingly streamlined girl who answered the phone, kept the sun-bed appointment schedule, and pre-sided over the check-in book. She sounded quite pleased to have a reason to approach Martin.

I ran upstairs, looked myself over in the mirror, and

decided that almost anything was good enough to run an errand with Sally. I brushed my hair quickly, securing it at the nape of my neck with a green band to match my T-shirt, and cleaned my Saturday glasses, huge ones with white-and-purple mottled frames.

Sally made a choking sound when she saw them. 'God Almighty, Roe, where'd you get those? You look like a clown.' She was shoveling papers and fast-food bags out of the passenger's seat of her car.

Talk about the honesty of friends.

'They're my Saturday glasses,' I said with dignity, locking my car and walking over to Sally's even older and more beat-up Toyota. The parking lot that served the newspaper staff was empty except for our cars and a Cadillac in the corner, which I recognized as the property of Macon Turner, owner and editor of the *Lawrenceton Sentinel*.

'Indicating that on Saturdays you are in a whoopee mood? Carefree and fun-loving?' Sally's voice was muffled as she bent back in. She'd opened a garbage bag and was swiftly sorting through the debris. Between the assorted paperwork, grocery bags, and cardboard cartons, I figured Sally had a whole tree in her front seat.

'Sorry about this,' she continued, as she emerged and carried the garbage bag over to the Dumpster. 'I have to do this under duress or not at all, and asking you to ride with me provided the duress.'

Sally was wearing slacks, which she seldom did on week-days, but her bronze curls and careful makeup were unchanging. Sally hadn't altered much in the years we'd been on-again, off-again friends. She'd had a wonderful but brief episode of gourmet cooking, tried marriage the same way, and now was back to Chick-Kwik, burgers, and the single life, without gaining a pound or wrinkling a crease. The only thing that made Sally look her age (which I estimated to be fifty-one) was her son, Perry.

I watched while Sally went down a mental checklist, giving a tiny nod as she reviewed each point on a list only she could see. Then she slid behind the wheel and said, 'Coming?'

Soon we were flying down the interstate, for Sally believed the speed limit was just a guideline. This belief accounted for Sally's knowing every highway patrolman in the area by his first name. But today, we weren't stopped, and we arrived at the Starry Night Airport having exchanged only a modicum of gossip.

We had left the interstate just five minutes east of Lawrenceton and had taken a state highway north a couple of miles, passing the usual seven million pine trees. Sally turned onto a road that scarcely deserved the name. It had been paved at one time, but that had been long ago. This alleged road terminated at the romantically named Starry Night Airport.

It was evident that Starry Night was a marginal business. Rendered invisible from the highway by a strip of pines and a ridge, the little airport had been carved out of the woods a long time ago. There were two runways, and even to my ignorant eyes it was apparent they were suitable only for small planes. Very small planes. The parking lot was small and graveled, delineated by landscape timbers. A concrete sidewalk led to the office, a little building about half the size of the ground floor of my house. This green-painted cement-block building had windows running nearly all the way around. Though the windows were curtained, the curtains were all wide open.

If you didn't turn off the sidewalk to enter the office, you continued past to the hangars. There were two. From the office, only the first few feet of the interior of each hangar would be visible. While both hangars were in use – I thought I could detect at least three tiny planes in the first, and two larger ones in the second – I couldn't see any people at all. Nothing moved.

I surveyed the grounds again. 'Now, wait a minute,' I said. Sally, who hadn't moved at all, looked at me with a little smile. 'You're wondering how the murderer got Jack's body to the plane?' she said.

I nodded. It would be brazen to carry the body to the plane past the open windows of the office, no matter how deserted the place seemed to be.

'Look,' she said, pointing out her window at a narrow gravel road, just wide enough for one vehicle, leading out of the parking lot and running up the ridge that rose behind the hangars.

'What about tracks?' I asked.

'No rain here for three weeks before Jack's body was dropped,' she said. 'The ground on either side of the gravel was rock-hard, so if there were tracks, they wouldn't amount to much. Now that we've had rain, it would be a different story.'

Instead of hopping out and going to the office, as I expected, Sally turned to me and said, 'Now, here's the reason I brought you along.'

I felt a warning bell go off in the 'better sense' area of my brain.

'Let's hear it,' I said, the caution in my voice making Sally purse her lips in exasperation.

'Well, Dan Edgar, the kid who wrote the story on the attack on Shelby, was too lazy to get out of bed this morning to help me, and the other reporters are all gone or sick this weekend.'

'So naturally you thought of me.' I raised one eyebrow, but possibly this effective expression was invisible behind my big glasses.

'Yes,' said Sally without a trace of irony. 'Actually, I did. You're small, you're quick, and if your husband's out of pocket, you're bored.'

'Well,' I said blankly, for want of something better.

'Anyway, this won't take long. Do you want to be the sneaker or the diversion?'

'How much trouble can I get into?'

'Oh, hardly any. I'll take responsibility.'

I tried raising the eyebrow again.

'Oh, okay, maybe yelled-at trouble, not jail trouble.'

I opted for the sneaker. I figured I already had so much trouble, a little more wouldn't make any difference.

'Okay,' Sally said. 'Now, here's what you have to do. When I was out here doing the story on Jack Burns, of course I asked the owner, an older guy named Stanford Foley, how it was possible for Jack and someone else to get in a plane without him even seeing it. He said it just couldn't happen, that he was here the whole time. The police can't make heads or tails of that, and I can't either.'

'Your story said Jack had rented the plane himself.'

'Yes, I said that, but I was counting on Foley too much. It turns out, Jack had reserved that time and that plane, but I don't think Foley saw him at all. I think Jack was brought here dead – he certainly wasn't killed in the plane, the cops tell me – and loaded into that plane by his killer. Jack's car was parked at the police station and nothing was wrong with it, so he didn't come here on his own and he wasn't killed in his own car.'

'So, what do you want me to do?'

'While I go in there and talk to Foley, I want you to sneak in that hangar and get in a plane. Actually, the plane that you saw that day, the one that transported the body, may be back here. It's one Mr Foley keeps to rent out to whoever wants it. Jack had actually flown it several times.'

Getting in a plane didn't sound too hard.

'According to your theory, the killer had Jack's body in the car and drove close to the hangar,' I said, feeling sure there was more to come.

'Well, right. Actually, that's what I want you to do, get the body to the plane. Just to prove it can be done without Mr Foley knowing anything at all. I want you to drive my car to the back of the first hangar – that's the one the plane Jack reserved was in – and drag the bag in my trunk down to the hangar. I want you to load that bag in a plane and get in yourself. You don't know how to fly a plane, do you? It would be great if you could actually take off without him knowing.'

'You should have asked Perry, he's taking lessons,' I reminded her, and she grimaced as if she'd bitten a lemon.

'Perry wouldn't do it, he'd just think of something else he had to do urgently,' Sally said. 'I don't know if Perry's so much learning how to fly a plane as learning how to fly Jenny Tankersley.'

I wasn't going to touch *that* one.

'So, just get the bag out of the trunk, down the hill, and into the plane,' Sally prompted.

This sounded trickier and trickier. 'How heavy a bag?' I asked, stalling for time.

'Oh. Pretty heavy – after all, it's supposed to be a body.'

'What if someone comes?'

'We'll just – tell them what we're doing!'

Sally seemed to think that would take care of everything. I was far from sure that was the case.

'Okay,' I said, hearing the doubt dripping from my voice.

'Good,' Sally said happily, gathering her purse and note-pad. 'I'll meet you back here. You have ten minutes, okay? And the object is not to let Foley see you. Or anybody else.'

Sally had made it sound like a kind of game, maybe a macabre version of hide-and-seek. But as soon as I began the experiment, it felt all too real. While Sally entered the office and hopefully began an intense conversation with Stanford Foley, I drove her old Toyota out of the parking lot and up the little graveled trail. The car lurched as I navigated it through the ruts, and my stomach began to match its motion.

I was up behind the first hangar in no time. I parked and got out, Sally's enormous bunch of keys hanging from my hand. No one ran out of the hangar or the office to demand an accounting of what I was doing. If I looked hard I could see Sally's head through one of the back windows of the office.

Time for phase two. I unlocked the trunk and stared at its contents with dismay. When Sally had said 'bag' I'd thought of a garbage bag filled with laundry or yard rakings. What

Sally had wedged in her trunk was an actual punching bag that she'd appropriated from someone's garage. The chain it had dangled from was still attached to three rings on the top of the bag, coming together to link on one large ring.

'Son of a *bitch*,' I said from the bottom of my heart. That certainly didn't mean anything in the context of my predicament, but it really made me feel better. 'Okay,' I said, trying to bolster my courage and muscle power. 'Okay, here we go.' And muttering further encouraging things and heaving with all my might, I got the punching bag out of the trunk.

If the chains hadn't been attached, Sally's little experiment would have ended right then and there. The only other way I could get the bag, which I estimated to weigh seventy pounds, down the slope would be to roll it. That would work with the bag, though the trip downhill might be rather uncontrollable, but with Jack's body it would not have done at all.

So I grabbed the chains, for after all, Jack could have been grabbed under the arms, and I dragged the bag downhill, feeling toward the end that my arms were going to come out of their sockets. I was quite certain that Sally owed me in a major way.

Halfway down the hill I achieved some self-knowledge. I would never have done this if I'd been single, because of the embarrassment of possibly being seen and questioned. But now that I was married to Martin, I was not so concerned. He gave me the confidence to do what I wanted to do, though it might be incredibly stupid. Like pulling a punching bag down a hill behind a very obscure little airport in northeast Georgia.

Then my foot touched concrete, and I realized I'd made it to the hangar. There was an enormous door right in the middle of the wall and it was wide open. Mr Foley was not a man to worry about security, despite what had happened the week before. Before I tried to get the bag in, I reconnoitered. The hangar, which felt cavernous, was full of shadows. The plane closest to the back door was green, but there were two little red-and-white ones, both with a Piper logo, either of which might have been the plane that dumped Jack Burns so unceremoniously into my yard. Though the concrete floor certainly had stains on it, the hangar was surprisingly neat, a credit to Mr Foley. There were shelves on the side, a little room in the corner, and metal drums holding rags and things I couldn't identify.

Well, the floor being clear was the main thing. I pulled the bag, which I was beginning to hate with all my might, across the smooth floor to the nearest of the red-and-white Pipers. It was unlocked, to my astonishment. I peered into the tiny cabin, feeling a little curious even though I knew I was supposed to be hurrying. I'd never seen the inside of a plane so small.

I hadn't been able to figure out how one person could fly the plane and dump the body out at the same time, but now that I could see the cabin, it was obvious that it would be easy. The pilot could lean across the body, which would be propped into the passenger's seat, open the passenger door, and give a good push, and the thing would be accomplished. It gave me the willies when I put Jack's face on the passenger, pictured it actually taking place.

Suddenly the loneliness of the hangar felt threatening rather than reassuring. I wanted to get the hell out of there.

What was a nice girl like me doing in a place like this? With a strength born of sheer exasperation, I hauled the bag to an upright position, squatted, embraced the bag, and lifted. I almost got it in the passenger's seat, but my height was the problem. Jack's assailant too must have had a terrible time unless he was at least a foot taller than me – lots of people were, of course.

I looked around desperately. There, some wooden pallets were stacked against the wall. I ran to get one, put the bag on it, stood on it myself, and with the extra height I managed to wrestle the bag into the plane. It was not sitting up neatly in the passenger's seat; it leaned awkwardly over into the pilot's side. But it was in the plane, as Sally had specified.

I returned the pallet, wiped the bag with a rag to remove my fingerprints (wondering all the while why I felt that was necessary), threw the rag back in the metal drum, and hightailed it out of the hangar.

I had to back down the track until I came to the point where it led down to the parking lot. There I was able to maneuver Sally's car to face downhill. Once I had her car back in its original position, I looked at my watch. Ten minutes, most of which had been absorbed by extricating the bag from the trunk, and hoisting the bag into the plane.

It felt like double that, I closed my eyes, scrunched down in the passenger's seat, and wondered if I could go to sleep. No, here came Sally accompanied by an older man who had a fine head of gray hair and an orange jumpsuit that looked quite good on him. An earphone set was around his neck, the little gray pads looking like buds on the ends of the metal arc. Wires led down to a tape player strapped to his waist, like the set Angel listened to so often while she did yard-work.

Sally was smiling and Stanford Foley was smiling, and I wondered if I was seeing the start of a Good Thing. The tall older man caught sight of me in the car, and said something to Sally, something on the order of 'Why didn't your friend come in?' because I could see the question on his face. Sally said something with a conspiratorial smile and he began laughing. I decided Sally's debt had just escalated.

She said a few more words, then traipsed down the sidewalk and slid into the car. Stanford Foley watched her with a happy face. I handed Sally the keys, and she started the motor under the watchful beam of her new swain.

When Sally had finished smiling and waving, and actually reversed the car, I asked in an acidic voice, 'When are you and Stanford going out?'

'Oh, Roe,' she said in a wounded way, 'can't I enjoy a man's company for just a little minute?'

'Not when I've been yanking my muscles all to pieces for you,' I said, and I meant it.

'So, tell me about it. How long did it take? I couldn't believe it when I looked out the window and the Toyota was back.' Sally could be tactful when she chose, and she could tell she'd better choose now.

I gave her as long an account of my ordeal as I could, since it had lasted only ten minutes.

'How'd you do with Mr Foley? Other than the obvious.'

'He's really a sweet guy. Did you know he lives in half of that little building? I think the line between being at home and off duty, and being at work and being alert, have kind of blurred for Stanford.'

'I saw he was wearing earphones.'

'That seems to be his main pleasure, listening to music on that Walkman set. He likes country and western.'

'He play it loud?'

'I got the feeling he does.'

'So did he even hear you park the car in the lot?'

'No.'

'Did he know I'd moved the car?'

'No.'

'Did he even look out in the lot and ask how you'd gotten out to the airport?'

'No. He was in the living quarters when I knocked on the door. He had the earphones on, and he was singing along with the tape. It took him forever to hear me. He never looked out the window the whole time I was there.'

'He could have missed the car or truck with Jack in it completely, then.'

Sally nodded, her attention focused on turning back onto the interstate.

'How does he know it was Jack who reserved the plane?' I asked.

'Jack called. He said to reserve the plane for ten o'clock on Monday morning. He asked if anyone else had reserved a plane for that morning, because he might have the Piper up for a while.'

'So Foley told him there were no more reservations.'

'Right.'

'How come Mr Foley's so sure it was Jack that called?'

Sally looked over at me sharply. 'Well, because that's who he said he . . . Oh.'

'Right. Who's to say it was Jack? Couldn't the killer have

made the reservation? All he'd have to know is that Jack used this airport.'

'You mean it was planned in advance.'

'Why not?'

Neither of us spoke for a minute, viewing with distaste bordering on nausea the murderer plotting with such care, perhaps seeing Jack often in the time between the call and the fall.

'Well,' said Sally, shaking herself and pulling out to pass a pickup that was surely going over the speed limit, 'I'll have to think about that some more. Later. Hey, I hear your friend Angel is pregnant!'

'Yes, she found out a few days ago.'

'That's great! Shelby Youngblood's pretty old to be a first-time dad, isn't he?'

'He's the same age as Martin.'

'Then you and Martin better get on the stick, girl. I had Perry so young that when I see these women having them late now, it seems funny to me. I know your mother would like a grandkid of her own – her husband's got three now, doesn't he?'

'She enjoys John's grandchildren a lot.' I turned to look out of the window at the secondhand car dealers and fast-food places that were beginning to line the road from the interstate to Lawrenceton.

'So what about your own?'

I kept my face averted. 'Sally, I can't have children.'

Horrified silence.

'Roe, I'm so sorry.' We'd come to a stoplight. Sally patted my hand, and I restrained the impulse to slap hers.

'You've checked with specialists, I'm sure.' Still, there was the question in her voice.

'Yes. I don't ovulate and I have a malformed womb.'

Laying it on the line.

'Roe, I don't know what to say, except I'm sorry.'

'That's all anyone can do,' I said, trying to keep the tears out of my voice.

'How long have you known?'

'Couple of months.'

'How's Martin reacting?'

I took a deep breath, trying to stay composed. This was too new a sore to touch without considerable pain. 'Martin wasn't sure he wanted more anyway. You know he has a son, Barrett, who's an adult now. So starting over had limited appeal for him.'

Sally finally seemed to realize I didn't want to stay on the subject. 'Well, I'll take you out to lunch when we get back, as a thank-you. And then I have to take the bag back. How about Beef 'N More?'

She pulled in neatly beside my car in the *Sentinel* parking lot.

I sat there with my eyes shut tight, waiting for the storm to begin.

I could feel Sally shift in her seat to look at me. She said sharply, 'What?'

'Um. The bag is still in the plane, Sally.'

'*What?*'

'You never said anything about putting it *back* in the car, Sally,' I said defensively. But I could feel the corners of my mouth turn up, and I was suppressing a laugh.

'Don't you dare smile! That was Sam Edgar's punching

bag! He gave me strict orders . . . you mean, it's still sitting in the airplane?' She couldn't quite believe me.

'Uh-huh.'

Unable to suppress it anymore, I began to laugh. After a second of staring at me with her mouth hanging open, Sally starting giggling, too.

'Which one is it in?' she gasped, wiping her eyes with the back of her hand.

'One of the little red-and-white ones.'

'Oh, dear. Oh no. How am I going to get it back? How am I going to explain it to Stanford?'

'Sally, my dear,' I said, sliding out of the Toyota, 'that is your problem. I guess our lunch is off now?'

Sally was shaking her head in exasperation, but still smiling a little, as I pulled out of the parking lot.

Martin was in the storage shed at the back of the garage when I got home. He had indeed been to the Athletic Club; he was still in his workout clothes.

Since he was soaked with sweat and smelled accordingly, maybe my hug was a little sketchy. 'I thought I'd finish mowing the yard,' he explained. 'You and Angel didn't get to finish last week, and the backyard looks . . . peculiar.'

It certainly did. I strolled across the covered walkway leading from our house to the garage, and looked at the yard for the first time since Jack Burns had made his re-entrance into my life. Martin had already been at work; I could see he'd filled the depression in the sod. You could see the mowed trail in the grass where Angel had let go of the lawn mower when I tackled her.

I shuddered, and was glad to answer Martin's irritable

call. He'd discovered the can of gas for the lawn mower was nearly empty, so I had to run back into town to get more. When I returned, I saw that Martin had gotten out the trimmer and started to clean up the edges of the yard and the tall grass around the stepping-stones in the front. The trimmer cord had gotten stuck and he was working over it with grim intensity.

'We are too used to having Shelby and Angel around,' Martin said, after struggling with the trimmer for several more silent, tense minutes. I'd been watching him work with, I hoped, an encouraging air, but I'd been contemplating retreating into the house on some pretext. I could tell Martin was very close to losing his temper, a rare and awful occurrence.

'I'll mow, if you want to keep working on that,' I said helpfully.

Martin told me in no uncertain terms that he never wanted to see the trimmer or touch it again as long as he lived.

I gathered that he would rather mow.

'Well, I'll fix lunch,' I offered, trying to think of something out of the ordinary that I could produce with speed.

'Only something light,' Martin said, pouring gas into the mower tank with the same concentration he did everything. 'Remember, we have the Pan-Am Agra banquet tonight.'

'Oh, right,' I said, trying not to sound as depressed as the thought made me feel.

The downside of being Martin's wife was having to attend so many *dinners*. We had to go to dinners in private homes given by plant officials, we had to go to annual dinners for the boards of this and that (naturally Martin was asked to sit on many boards), we had to go to charity fund-raising dinners . . . the list went on and on. And since Martin was a vice president of Pan-Am Agra, the highest-ranking local executive, I was expected to be the first lady, so to speak.

I am naturally polite and have decent table manners since my mother brought me up right. And I like to wear pretty clothes and get some attention, because I am a human being. But the constant feeling of being under observation, the anxiety that I might embarrass Martin, and above all the numbing sameness of these events, had dimmed my enthusiasm pretty quickly.

I trailed into the kitchen to make a fruit salad and checked my calendar. Yes, I'd written in the dinner and at the same time had made an appointment with Benita at the Clip Casa to have my hair put up, and I had to be there in twenty-two minutes.

I chopped fruit with vigor, left the kitchen in a mess, and yelled to Martin out the back door to let him know where I was going. Martin had left the garage door open since he'd been tinkering with the trimmer, and Madeleine, as always, had taken advantage of the situation to put paw prints on Martin's Mercedes. I told her again how stupid that was, wiped off the paw prints with a rag, ejected the cat from the garage, backed my car out, and pressed the automatic closer while Madeleine was still sulking on the stairs to the Young-bloods' apartment.

Benita was idly picking at her orange hair when I hurried in the door. I was four minutes late, and on a Saturday that was a sin. But I was contrite enough to talk her back into a good humor and she so seldom saw me that she had a great fund of family happenings to relate.

The beauty shop atmosphere was soothing, and my muscles, strained from their session with the punching bag, let me know they were glad to rest. The smell of the chemicals and the pastel decor, Benita's drawl, and the drone of the hair dryer made me feel sleepy and content. Benita decided my ends needed trimming, took care of that, and began the long process of putting my mass of hair up. All I needed to do was say 'Really?' or 'Oh yes,' from time to time. I flipped through a magazine, as always surprised and a little dismayed at what other females apparently found interesting – or at least the publishers thought they would – and planned what I'd wear that night. A few other women connected with the Pan-Am Agra plant came into Clip Casa to get beautified for the banquet, and I was polite to everyone, but I didn't feel like talking and didn't initiate any conversation.

By the time I left the beauty parlor it was late in the afternoon.

I cautiously surveyed the backyard and observed it had been mowed and trimmed. With considerable relief, I went in the kitchen door, and found the kitchen completely clean. I crossed the hall to the study, and found Martin wrapped in his golden brown terry robe, watching the news. He switched off the set and got up to give me a kiss and walk around me to view my hair. Benita had slicked it back, braided it, and wound the braid into a knot at the nape of my neck.

'You look great,' Martin murmured, closing in from

behind to kiss my neck. I shivered pleasantly and we both looked at the clock on Martin's desk.

'Will you be careful of my hair?' I asked strictly.

'As careful as can be,' Martin said, not letting up on the neck work.

'Beat you up the stairs,' I said.

But gee, he caught me.

Chapter Eight

We had to get there early to meet and greet, but we found time to stop by the hospital. Shelby expected to be discharged the next day, and Martin promised to help, after he had a good look at Angel. She was obviously uncomfortable and exhausted after sleeping on the lumpy roll-away the hospital had provided. Shelby told us with more than a hint of exasperation that he'd urged her repeatedly to sleep at home.

Jimmy Henske had been by that day to question him again, but Shelby said he'd had to tell Jimmy that he still could not recall why he'd been roaming around the yard on a black rainy night, what he might have seen, who might have hit him.

Shelby's room was pleasantly cluttered with offerings from the men he worked with; paperbacks, sports magazines, a basket of fruit, and some get-well cards jostled each other for space on the broad windowsill.

As Martin and I made our unnecessarily complicated way out of the hospital (I wondered if the architect had just read a book on English mazes before he began on the hospital plans) and into the overcrowded parking lot, I noticed I was again experiencing the unease I'd had earlier, the chill of loss, as though the Youngbloods, bound to us by employment and friendship, were moving away from us for good.

I was in no party mood when we pulled into the parking lot of the community center. Martin cut off the motor and we sat looking at the concrete-and-glass building, the fresh-painted parking lot with its rudimentary trees in the medians. We heaved simultaneous sighs.

'We'll get through it,' Martin said bracingly.

'I know.' But I heard the complaint in my voice and said, 'At least we get to look marvelous for the evening! And I'm looking forward to seeing so many of the people I only get to see at Pan-Am Agra things.'

Martin hated being part of a receiving line, so we just happened to be close to the entrance; anyone who felt like it could shake Martin's hand or hug my neck, or give us both stiff bobs of the head. I resigned myself to being called 'Mrs Bartell' all evening, since the constant correction 'Ms Teagarden' would have been tedious.

For this annual occasion, Pan-Am Agra had rented the newly built community center, which boasted a huge room that could be adapted to many purposes. This evening it looked festive, with giant Easter eggs and streamers and balloons combating the general institutional atmosphere. A potted bare artificial tree stood in the middle of the room with large plastic eggs hanging from it, each containing a slip of paper describing a door prize. I'd already been informed I was the designated distributor, and I watched with resignation as the glass bowl by the entrance filled with more and more slips with names scrawled on them, as more and more Pan-Am Agra employees slapped on their hand-lettered name stickers and moved into the room.

This was supposed to be a dressy occasion; but as always, nowadays, there were people who came in blue jeans or stretch pants. My mother would have shuddered. I felt grateful I'd dressed down in a rather plain cocktail dress in cream and gold. I was wearing heels, which I hated with a passion, and every time my feet throbbed I told myself this was my sacrifice for Martin, a return for all the times he took it for granted I would go my own way and do whatever made me happiest.

I caught glimpses of my husband surrounded by men in suits who were laughing, holding glasses of nonalcoholic punch (Pan-Am Agra could not support drinking and driving), and from time to time glancing over to the tables where their wives were already seated. Martin was at ease, dealing with the conversation with good humor and a natural facility.

I wasn't faring as well. I was getting a bit tired of so many women telling me in so many words that I was lucky to have such a handsome husband. If Martin and I had been the same age, they wouldn't have commented; I couldn't quite work out why the age difference apparently gave them license to speak frankly. I was willing to bet none of the men were complimenting Martin on my big boobs.

Every now and then, I'd get to talk to someone I really liked, like Martin's secretary, Mrs Sands, a tall, thin forty-five with luridly dyed black hair and a broad sense of humor. Tonight, I could only view Mrs Sands with awe. She was decked out in a red-and-gold sequined sweater, red slacks, and gold sandals with three-inch heels that made her even loftier. My own modest heels looked sedate in comparison. Mrs Sands, Marnie to her friends (but not to me), gave me the dignified greeting one potentate accorded another of slightly greater stature. Though I was the sultan's wife, her manner implied, she was the Grand Vizier, the one who held true power.

Actually, she was right in many ways. I didn't mind giving her credit; Martin said she was a great secretary, gauging perfectly when to allow plant personnel to have access to him, when to leave him undisturbed, and how to locate him at any moment.

'Honey,' said Mrs Sands, 'I need to talk to you.' She glanced around; we were a little apart at the moment. I looked up at her, surprised and interested; usually we just exchanged compliments and small talk.

'Fire away,' I said.

'Now, I know Mr Bartell is a man who can handle any situation, that's one of the reasons I like working for him, but you're his wife and there's something building up out there I think you ought to know about.'

Mrs Sands cocked her head and her teased black hair leaned a little, like a loose helmet. She was deeply tanned and the wrinkles around her dark brown eyes looked as though they'd been incised with a chisel.

'Tell me,' I said invitingly.

'You know Bettina Anderson?'

'Yes. We had supper at Bettina and Bill's house one time. Oh, and she left a couple of messages on my answering machine I haven't had a chance to return,' I recalled guiltily. As a matter of fact, the dinner at the Andersons' had been the first one Martin and I had attended as a married couple; and it had been the first evening I'd realized that the future held many such unwanted but obligatory invitations.

Bill Anderson, the plant safety manager, had been wished on Martin by his superiors. The Andersons had been in

Lawrenceton about three years. Bettina, a stout copper-haired woman of about forty, was the most self-effacing wife I'd ever encountered. 'I haven't seen either of the Andersons in a few months, I guess,' I said lamely, aware that Mrs Sands was waiting for me to say something more.

'Well, I think she's going through some kind of thing about Mr Bartell. I can't *believe* she's tried to call you!'

My mouth fell open.

'Bettina Anderson, who's married to Bill, head of the Safety Division,' I said, just a little question in my voice, because I simply couldn't believe my ears.

'That's right, I can't believe it either,' Mrs Sands said, responding to my tone and my statement at the same time.

I looked down at my shoes, off-white leather with a gold cap over the toes. I bit my lip to keep from giggling.

'Mr Bartell usually handles situations like this himself, he sure don't need help with that,' Mrs Sands continued, and I abruptly lost any tendency to laugh. I wondered how many other 'situations' Martin had handled without my knowledge. I could see how it would be hard for him to say casually, 'Fended off another admirer, honey.'

'But this time, this woman is acting so weird, and so's her husband,' Mrs Sands said, disgust in her stance. 'Weird' was one of the worst epithets Mrs Sands ever used, and she did not use it lightly.

'Weird in what way?' I asked, returning my gaze to my shoes. This conversation was embarrassing, but fascinating.

'Well, Bill shows up at times when he doesn't really need to see Mr Bartell.' My husband was the only 'Mister' at the Pan-Am Agra plant, to Mrs Sands. 'He just hangs around until Mr Bartell gets rid of him – you know how quick he can do that.'

I nodded. I did indeed.

'And Bettina?' I prompted.

'Honey, that woman calls on the phone, and she's come to the office! Course, I told her he was out of town.'

'Oh, dear,' I said inadequately.

'Now that you know, I feel better,' Mrs Sands told me. 'I'll be seeing you, Ms Teagarden.' Mrs Sands always gave me the correct name, but accompanied it by a sharp look. Keeping my name had cost me many points with Mrs Sands, but she was trying to forgive me, since I seemed like a proper wife for Mr Bartell. She gave my shoulder a squeeze and strode off to join a group of her cronies, who'd been glancing our way.

Before I had a chance to recover from this remarkable conversation, before I could even wiggle my eyebrows at Martin to indicate I wanted to talk to him, the Andersons came in the door. Bill was wearing a suit, of course, and Bettina was wearing a very pretty green dress. When she shyly eased in front of me, I was able to give her an honest compliment. Bettina smiled back uncertainly. I noticed her hands were twisting the strap of her purse.

I emitted some more social chitchat, which Bettina interrupted abruptly. 'Could we talk tonight? It won't take long. I'm sorry I have to talk to you here, but you didn't return my calls. Of course,' and she held up a hand to ward off my speaking, 'I understand, because you've had a lot of things to think about lately. But I have to talk to you tonight.' She had spoken in a low urgent voice, with a glance toward our husbands that certainly must have clued any onlooker that she was up to something surreptitious. Of course in such a throng some people were sure to be looking at us, and I tried to make my face as blank as possible.

'Sure, Bettina,' I said, as soothingly as I could without sounding patronizing. 'What about right now?'

'Oh no, people are looking, and it's just about time to sit down.' So she was having that watched feeling, too.

'This is awfully crowded,' I said. 'Why don't we have lunch Monday?' If I could get through this evening, I could surely endure a public lunch with Bettina Anderson.

'That's too late, I can't wait that long,' Bettina told me. There was an edge of desperation in her voice that I couldn't ignore.

'All right. When the dinner is breaking up, come to our table and we'll find a quiet place.'

And then I had to put on my social smile, because here came (to my dismay) Deena Somebody-who-worked-in-the-shipping-department. Deena had deemed skin-tight jeans appropriate for this occasion, and I had to admit she filled them beautifully, but I had doubts that she would be able to bend at her knee and hip joints to sit in one of the folding chairs. I would have been interested in a video of the process of Deena getting into those jeans. Deena shrieked, 'Hello, Roe!' as if she were a close friend of mine, and hauled her date out to show me she had one. To my amazement, the man she had in tow was quiet Paul Allison.

'Hi, Roe,' said Paul in his calm way. 'I'm sure you know Deena Cotton.' I must have been fascinated by Deena's bottom half for too long – she was eyeing me nervously.

'Deena, how's shipping these days?' I murmured, proving I recognized her and knew where she worked.

'Just fine, always busy. Thank goodness!' And Deena gave a high-pitched giggle that made me wonder just how far Paul was willing to go in reaction to Sally, who would never in her life have made a sound like that. He was willing to go pretty far, as it turned out, for he put his hand firmly on her butt while we talked, and she seemed pleased rather than annoyed. I tried to imagine getting out of clothes that tight in the heat of passion; just as I had decided Paul would have to stand at the end of the bed and pull on the legs as she held on to the headboard, I became aware that Deena had turned red and Paul was staring at me fixedly, waiting for me to speak.

'Hope you enjoy yourselves tonight,' I said briskly.

I looked down rather than show my irritation, pushed my wire-rims up with one finger to give myself an excuse for glancing away. 'Perry,' I said over Paul's shoulder, 'Good to see you.' To my surprise, Paul's former stepson had come in right behind him with a woman who must be the remarkable Jenny Tankersley. Paul and Deena were moving away, and I tried not to even glance at the rear view.

'Jenny's airstrip is where the Pan-Am Agra plane lands when the president flies down,' Perry was explaining. 'This is the second year Jenny's been invited to the banquet.'

I didn't remember her from the year before, but perhaps she just hadn't come up to meet me. I was sure I would have had no trouble recognizing her if I'd been introduced. Jenny, who was the same height as Perry, had gleaming beautiful white teeth, which she frequently bared in a predatory smile. Her hair was cut very short, with bangs, and it was a glossy brown that contrasted well with her heavy gold jewelry and orange dress. I had heard many stories about this woman, and I was interested in talking to her, but now was not the time to get to know her better.

I said a few polite words, to which Jenny responded instead of Perry, and then the younger couple drifted off to sit with Paul and Deena Cotton. I noted that Deena had somehow managed to sit, but she was bolt upright.

I assessed the incomings – down to a trickle – and the seated employees – a great majority – and knew it was time for the banquet to officially begin. Martin met my eye, with his usual good timing, and together we glanced around for seats, which would be simply the first two side-by-side we saw. At the annual banquet, Martin and I were supposed to be just part of the gang, with the result that some plant workers were in for a very tense evening sitting with the boss.

I spotted a table about fifteen yards away, and as Martin and I made our way there we passed a head of pale curly hair I thought I recognized. When I glanced back in amazement, I confirmed my suspicion; Arthur Smith was there with another woman, this one a very young twenty-something with her hair actually in a ponytail.

I looked straight into his eyes, which were focused on me, gave him some anger in the look, and turned my face to my husband.

Of course, Martin hadn't missed it. 'What the hell is he doing here?' he murmured through a genial smile. Martin and Arthur had always had a profound dislike of each other.

'He and Lynn have separated.'

'So he's out with a woman half his age?'

I wisely said nothing. I didn't think the woman was *that* young, but she was maybe fifteen years younger than Arthur, who was about thirty-four. I didn't think it was the right time to remind Martin he was fifteen years older than I.

'Are Lynn and Arthur going to get divorced?' Martin asked, sliding my chair out for me while nodding at the others seated at the table, who were displaying an interesting variety of reactions to the presence of the boss and his wife.

'I hope not, for the sake of the little girl,' I said. 'And it would be his second divorce.'

Then we had to drop our own conversation and tend to our social duties. Martin knew the name of every worker at our table, and met their spouses with great aplomb. I didn't have that gift, but I worked hard, and I hoped not obviously, at matching Martin's geniality and his easy conversation.

Every time I had to go to an affair like this one, my earnest prayer was that I would think at least once before I spoke, twice if possible. I didn't want to provide fodder for any amusing anecdotes.

I discussed school-system problems with a mother of three, sewing one's own clothes with another woman, and planting roses with another. I plowed steadily through the evening, eating little of the barbecued chicken and slaw, but doing my corporate duty. When the Employee Services man, who had to act as MC on these occasions, stood up to tell a few jokes and introduce Martin, I sighed a silent breath of relief.

Martin rose to the occasion with a few well-chosen words about the increased productivity at the plant, his goals for the year, and the pride he took in working with such a fine group of people. He went on about how he'd taken Georgia to his heart, turning this into a reference to his marriage to a true Georgia peach; and then he concluded neatly, pleasing those who had come with any tendency to be pleased.

I kept my face turned toward Martin and an indulgent smile pasted on my lips, but I was more interested in scanning the faces I knew in the crowd. Paul was looking at Martin, but as if he weren't really seeing him. It was obvious that his thoughts were far away. Perry was not paying any attention at all; if I was right, he and Jenny were up to something under the tablecloth. And Arthur was neglecting his young date to glare at Martin as though my husband were saying derogatory things about Arthur's ancestry. Marnie Sands was listening to make sure her boss did her proud, and the Andersons were whispering anxiously to each other.

Martin gave me my cue as name-drawer for the door prizes, all donated from local businesses that Pan-Am Agra patronized heavily. There were ten prizes to distribute this year, and I had to reach in the bowl, draw out a slip with a name scrawled on it, and search the crowd for whoever looked happy when I called the name. Then I unhooked the string attaching one of the giant eggs to the tree and handed it to the winner, who was supposed to open the egg on the spot so everyone could admire the donated largesse. It was kind of nice to be able to give people things that made them happy, especially at no expense to myself, and I enjoyed this part of the evening, though deciphering the scribbled signatures on the slips of paper could sometimes be a problem.

One of the recipients happened to be seated at Arthur's table, and as I called the man's name I noticed that Arthur was staring at me as if he hadn't eaten his dinner and I was a barbecued chicken breast.

I had the strongest yearning for a water gun.

At last, the evening dragged to an official end. The couples we'd been sitting with said ceremonious goodbyes, Martin excused himself to congratulate the Employee Services man on his organization of the event, and I was alone for the first time in what felt like years. I surreptitiously opened my compact below the table level to check my face for wear and tear, discovered a crumb of roll on my cheek that must have been there for an hour, and took care of that little problem. I spotted a clean napkin and polished my glasses, wondering how long the E.S. man would keep Martin talking, and if there were actually blisters on my feet. And then I was no longer alone.

True to her word, here was Bettina Anderson, who had fared even worse than I in terms of visible wear – she had a prominent grease stain on the skirt of her green dress. She was just as tense, just as wired up, as she had been earlier in the evening.

I felt sorry for her, and very wary.

'You have to help me, Aurora,' she said earnestly. Her heavy mouth had lost its lipstick and her nose needed powder. She clutched my arm, and I gritted my teeth to endure the contact.

'Tell me what's wrong,' I said evenly.

'Jack Burns died in your yard. Did he say anything before he died?'

Back to Jack Burns again. I tried not to see him falling. His funeral was tomorrow, and I dreaded the thought of it. 'No,' I said wearily. 'Bettina, I'm sure he was dead when he fell. He couldn't have said anything.' She looked unconvinced. Stung clean out of courtesy, I said, 'And besides, what business is it of yours?'

'I'm so scared,' she said. Now *that* I believed; I could feel her fear.

'He knew about us,' she said. For one horrifying moment I thought she meant Jack Burns had knowledge of an affair between Bettina and my husband.

Then I was back in my right mind and I put a couple of things together.

'Is your husband the one in the Federal Witness—?'

'Hush! Hush!'

I looked around. There was no one within ten feet.

'How'd you find out about that?'

'That was just the rumor . . .'

'Someone's talking, oh, God!'

'So John *is* the one?'

'Not John! Me!'

'What—?'

'I was the bookkeeper for one of the shell businesses run by Johnny Marconi.'

'Wow.' I gaped at this ordinary woman who had helped bring down a vicious man involved in peddling every kind of vice, a man who was a murderer many times over.

'So did they find out from Jack before he died who we were, where we were?' She stared at me as if she could will me to know the answer.

'I don't know,' I said, wishing I had a better reply to give her.

'Dryden can't find out, no one can find out, and we sit every night and wait for them to come.'

'Mr Dryden must have seen the autopsy reports,' I said. 'Did they show Jack was tortured before he fell?'

'No. But some things would have been obliterated by the fall,' she said. 'And they might have threatened him with a knife or something, without actually using it, before they killed him.'

I cast around to think of something comforting to tell this woman.

'They would have come by now if Jack had told them,' was the best I could come up with. I tried to picture Mafia hit men from Chicago traveling to Lawrenceton, Georgia – asking questions at the Shop-So-Kwik. My mind boggled.

'Did your husband work for Pan-Am Agra in Chicago?' I asked.

She stared at me for a moment. 'No, but he had a similar job at a similar company, and he was familiar with Pan-Am Agra's benefits, and he knew they had a plant down here and another in Arkansas. Either would have done, but it happened they needed a safety director here, so it was arranged. No one locally knew who we really were, except Jack Burns. Or so we thought.'

This was all as interesting as could be, but I became aware that her husband and my husband were waiting for us, making weary conversation. If Bill Anderson had wanted to have the same conversation with Martin that his wife was having with me, he showed no signs of it now. Martin saw me look at him, and wiggled his watch arm, his signal that he really wanted to leave.

'I wish I could tell you something either way,' I said honestly.

'Dryden doesn't think we've been compromised. But

we're going on vacation, starting tomorrow, and the watch will be kept for anyone asking questions. We'll be back. I would hate to move, but we just may have to. You know,' she added as she rose to her feet, 'if you tell anyone about this, we may end up getting killed. I tried to talk to your husband, but I think he could tell we had secrets, because he wouldn't meet with me privately, and Bill couldn't make up his mind whether or not it was a good idea to talk to Martin. He figured that anything you knew, you would have told your husband, and he knows Martin better; and I'd just met you that one time, at our house. Now you know about us, and our lives are your property. But I had to ask if you knew anything, had seen anything. We have to know. We just have to.'

And without further ado she walked slowly away, a stout red-haired woman in fear for her life, whom I'd always known as the boring and self-effacing Bettina Anderson. She put her hand on her husband's arm, said something to him quietly, and Bill shook hands with Martin in leave-taking.

I wondered what her christened name was. I wondered how her husband felt about hiding with his wife. I wondered if they had grown children in Chicago, what those children had been told.

'What was that all about?' Martin asked. I'd been so preoccupied I hadn't noticed him approaching, and I jumped. 'They've been asking me weird questions for a week,' he continued, 'and wanting to meet with me privately without either one of them telling me why. After Bill was foisted on me by the Chicago guys, I smelled something strange about the Andersons, and I just don't want to be involved in whatever trouble they're in . . . after all my own problems with our government.' We exchanged a look; that was a time we didn't talk about anymore.

'I thought maybe she had a thing for you,' I confessed.

'I was worried about that, too,' he admitted. 'Though it didn't have that feel . . . but all the secrecy. So, are you going to tell me?'

'I don't know,' I said, dismay showing in my voice. 'I don't know if I can.' I couldn't think of anything I'd ever withheld from Martin in our two years together, but I couldn't dismiss Bettina's plea for secrecy either.

'Can I think about it?' I asked Martin.

'Sure. I often feel I know more about my employees' private lives than I want to know, anyway.' But I could tell by the set of his shoulders that he was piqued with me.

As we neared the exit (Martin good-byeing right and left to people who'd lingered to talk) we came face-to-face with Arthur Smith and his ponytailed date. Martin's hand gripped mine more tightly. 'Hello, Sue,' Martin said to the girl. 'How are you?'

'Fine, Mr Bartell,' she said self-consciously. 'Have you met Arthur Smith?'

The silence held on too long for even young Sue to ignore. 'So you guys have met,' she said nervously, finally aware there was something going on.

Martin and I gave Arthur identical stiff nods, and Martin said, 'Night, Sue. See you in Ag Products tomorrow.' Martin held open one of the glass doors for me, and I stepped out into the cool evening air. Martin appeared beside me again, and took my hand. I heard the door swoosh shut, and then open again for young Sue and Arthur.

We stepped into a knot of people who had been tempted by the beautiful evening to linger to chat on the sidewalk; Perry and Jenny Tankersley, Paul and Deena Cotton, Marnie Sands (who seemed to be groping for something in her purse). Bill and Bettina Anderson had been waylaid by one of Martin's division heads, a balding paunchy man named Jesse Prentiss, who was introducing his wife Verna.

Just at that moment all hell broke loose, all hell in the form of a swift and terrified gray cat that streaked across the circles of light and dark dappling the parking lot, a cat hotly pursued by a large and shaggy dog with a length of frayed rope flying from its collar.

There was a hoot of laughter here and there, an exclamation of alarm from those who couldn't immediately see what was causing the hoopla, and a few halfhearted attempts to call the dog or grab the length of rope. The scene drew the stragglers in the parking lot together in a loose knot. After a moment the animals were gone, continuing their chase into the modest residential area on the next street. The yelping of the dog was still clear.

My eyes, like everyone else's, had followed the cat, who'd bounded onto and then over a car parked in the shadows at the very far reaches of the community center lot. I listened with half my attention to the comments and jokes the incident had sparked in the little crowd, while trying to figure out if I had indeed seen a blond head in the car that the cat had cleared in her escape.

Sure enough, I caught a glimpse of blond again, and one of the sodium lights caught a gleam of glasses.

Well, well. To cap off a jarring evening, who did I spy lurking in the parking lot but Mr Dryden. Agent Dryden?

Marshal Dryden? Even his protectee had only called him 'Dryden'.

Was he waiting to see if anyone followed the Andersons? Or was he watching us?

I was so engrossed in my thoughts in the seconds following the animals' exit from the parking lot that I was taken utterly by surprise by the sudden pressure on my back.

I heard a woman scream. My hand was ripped from its loose grip with Martin's.

To my bewilderment I found myself being pressed down to the ground by a warm weight that I could not support, though my feet shuffled for balance and my knees braced to push back. I heard another shriek, and thought *That wasn't me,* and a deep groan followed by a curse, all in the second that this inexorable, inexplicable weight drove me to the pavement. I threw my hands out in front of me to break my fall, but even my braced arms couldn't stop my cheek from hitting the sidewalk.

In the long, long minute before the weight was lifted, as I lay prone under the terrifying burden, I felt something wet on my face and opened my eyes to see blood dripping to the gleaming new sidewalk a half-inch from my nose.

After a frantic little inventory of pains, I was pretty sure it wasn't my blood.

Out of a cacophony of voices I discerned Paul Allison bellowing for calm, and I could hear one woman set up a steady howl for help – Bettina Anderson, I thought. 'Ready on three,' I heard Martin say, and the shuffle of feet all around me. 'One, two, three!' Martin said, and the weight on top of me was eased off. I had had the breath knocked out of me, and was frantically trying to take in air, with the usual result that I was foiling my own attempt.

I saw some knees hit the pavement beside me.

'Don't move,' Martin said tensely. 'Baby, is anything broken? Are you hurt?' Struggling for breath, I couldn't answer.

'Call 911!' exclaimed a male voice, Jesse Prentiss's, I thought. 'You! Perry Allison! There's a phone in the manager's office to the left of those glass doors!' Running feet, light; Perry pounding obediently into the community center.

Running feet, heavy. 'Who got hurt?' Dryden, breathing raggedly. So I'd been right; he'd been parked at the far reaches of the lot.

'Move back, people, police are on the way,' Paul Allison said loudly in his police official voice. 'I've already radioed from my car. Step back, everyone, unless you're an EMT.'

'I am,' Jenny Tankersley was saying as I felt Martin's hands running over my body.

'Then get over here,' Martin snapped, and Paul Allison said in a shocked voice, 'Has Roe been hurt?'

'She took a fall, she's okay,' Dryden said – rather cavalierly, I thought. 'But this man here is really bleeding.'

'There's blood on Roe,' Paul pointed out tensely.

And then I could breathe. Nothing had felt as good in weeks as that deep intake of air.

'I'm okay,' I croaked. 'Just help me up, Martin. I don't think it's my blood.'

I managed to push up with my arms to achieve a kneeling position, and then Martin lifted me up the rest of the way, frantically touching my head and neck to see where I'd been hurt.

We were a little apart from the activity now, which was centered on someone lying on the ground. The girl with the ponytail, Sue, was sobbing hysterically by one of the lampposts. 'He just fell down,' she said over and over, 'he just let go of my arm and fell down.'

'Not my blood,' I reassured Martin. This time he listened.

'Tell me how you're feeling,' he said.

'I bumped my cheek on the pavement,' I gasped. I took another deep breath and started again. 'I'm going to have sore hands and arms from trying to stop my fall, and my knees are scraped. Other than that, I'm fine. How'd I get knocked down?'

'Something happened to Arthur Smith,' Martin said slowly, his eyes never leaving my face. 'He was right behind you. Without any warning, he began to fall, and fell on you and took you down with him.'

'Did he have a heart attack?' No, the blood. 'Was he shot? How could he have been hurt?'

'Here comes the ambulance,' Martin said. 'Maybe we'll find out.'

Jenny Tankersley had been working on Arthur, ripping off his shirt to find the source of the bleeding, checking his pulse. The EMTs pelted out of the ambulance.

'He's been hurt on his shoulder somehow,' she told them, moving aside. No one was talking to Arthur himself, though I could see his eyes were open and he was taking in what was going on around him. He looked as dazed as I felt. But when his eyes focused on the first man out of the ambulance, Arthur seemed to collect himself. He said clearly, 'Murray, I was stabbed in the shoulder.'

*

A hush fell over the little crowds. Martin put his arm around me and I leaned on his chest. I had a moment of thankfulness that Martin had been holding my hand when the attack on Arthur occurred, so it was out of the question that Martin could have been involved. Not that he would do anything like that, but other people, knowing of the dislike between them, might make something of Martin's proximity.

Then I realized what must have already occurred to everyone there. If Arthur had been stabbed instead of shot, it had to have been by one of the people in the small cluster on the sidewalk.

As the ambulance rolled off with Arthur in the back, the Prentisses offered Sue a ride home.

'I'm afraid we're all going to have to stay here for a while,' Paul said in his calm way, and to reinforce his words, two police cars flew into the parking lot, shortly to be followed by two more.

A police detective was down, and this made the second officer in a week who'd been attacked. Before the evening was over, I'd seen every member of the force come and go at the community center.

We were all searched, even me, which made no sense at all, as Martin pointed out several times.

'Martin, I don't mind,' I told him wearily, as I got up to go to the women's room with a female officer – thankfully, not Lynn Liggett Smith. 'I just want to get this over with and go home.'

So off I trudged, my little evening bag tucked under my arm, to submit my bag and my body to an examination.

No knife or any other pointed object was found on any person in the group.

It was as if a knife had fallen from the sky, stabbed Arthur in the shoulder, and been pulled back up by an invisible cord.

Chapter Nine

I woke in the morning to a warm bed, Martin still asleep beside me, and rain lashing around the house outside. I peeked at the clock on my bed table; only seven-thirty. Plenty of time to get ready for church at nine-thirty. I squirmed over to press against Martin.

He's a quick waker. As soon as I heard his breathing change he turned over and put an arm around me.

'Martin, about last night,' I said, my voice still heavy with sleep.

'Not right now,' he whispered, his hands beginning to travel.

'Ummmm,' was the next thing I said, and then I didn't say any more for a good few minutes.

In fact, I didn't say one coherent word until Martin was coming out of the shower I'd previously vacated. As I was tucking my beige-and-black silk blouse into my long beige skirt, I gave him an exaggerated leer. He held up a hand in protest, which caused the bath towel to droop interestingly.

'Don't even think of it,' he said. 'Remember my advanced age.'

I laughed, and began brushing my hair. 'I'm pretty sure I could overcome your feebleness,' I said. 'But I don't want to be late for church. Of course, there's all afternoon. . .'

'So you're not going to the funeral?'

'Oh, shoot.' I put my brush down and made a face into the mirror. 'I wish you hadn't reminded me. I guess I could think of an excuse, but I really ought to go. After all, he fell into our yard. I think that obliges me.'

'You Southerners have the strangest sense of obligation,' Martin observed.

He didn't often begin a sentence that way, so I forgave him.

'I know you have to go get Shelby, so you won't be thinking about going to church,' I said carefully. 'Do you think you'll be home in time for the funeral? Do you even want to go?'

'I should go out to the plant for a while,' he said, pulling on his left sock, 'especially since I was gone for a couple of days this week.' I tried not to let my face fall. Martin felt he had to go in to work most weekends.

'I'll try not to stay long,' he continued.

I made a resigned face at my reflection and rummaged among the lipstick tubes in my dressing table drawer. But I wouldn't change the sheets; I still had a faint hope that later in the day it would prove to have been wasted effort. Actually, I'd settle for sitting in the same room while we read. Though our sex life was often wonderful, our 'together' time was minimal. I scanned the closet for my black pumps and slid my bare feet into them.

'No hose?' Martin said as he zipped up his blue jeans. He reached in a drawer to pull out a T-shirt. He seldom got to dress this casually.

'My knees have scabs from hitting the sidewalk last night, in case you didn't notice. And they're pretty sore.'

'Oh, honey, did I hurt you? Earlier?'

'If you did I didn't notice! But now that I'm up and around, I can tell I hit the pavement.' I flexed my leg and winced.

'Maybe while I'm at the hospital I'll check to see how Arthur Smith is,' Martin said, with a marked lack of enthusiasm.

'That would probably be good for appearances, anyway,' I said. 'Thank God you were holding my hand when he was stabbed . . . or whatever happened to him.'

Martin stood behind me and bent to kiss my neck at the spot that always makes me gasp. 'Some people that you dated, being around them doesn't bother me. But being around Arthur does, not because I think you have feelings for him but because he must still have some for you. He always gives me this look, "I had her first, I know all about the mole on her back", crap like that. And once Lynn and he have separated, what does he do? Puts himself right in your line of vision and looks at you as if he was a painter and you were the Mona Lisa.'

'And gets stabbed,' I said, to point out that Arthur's evening hadn't ended well, however much staring he'd done. I polished my black oblong-framed glasses, the ones I almost always wore to church, since they made me look serious. I peered into the mirror to check my makeup and decided I was entirely too pale. Maybe this year, for the first time since I was a teenager, I'd try to get a tan. If I went about it carefully, perhaps the sun wouldn't hurt my skin too badly. 'You know, Martin, I'd think I had it worked out if it wasn't for Arthur,' I said, pulling a Kleenex out of its box to blot my lipstick.

Martin, bent over to tie his Avias, said, 'What? You worked out what?'

'All this violence.'

'What's your theory?' Martin leaned his elbows on his knees to listen.

'I think it's because of Angel.'

Martin was astonished. 'How do you figure that?'

'Okay,' I said, holding up my fingers. 'Jack Burns's body was dropped in the yard while she was out mowing.'

Martin nodded cautiously.

'Then Beverly was rude to Angel in the library, and Beverly got attacked.'

I was busy folding fingers down and Martin was nodding.

'Then Beverly's purse was found on Angel's car.'

'What does that mean?'

'Whoever did it was saying to Angel, "Look what I did for you!" Like Jack's body falling in her yard. Just like Madeleine.'

Martin raised his eyebrows, as if to say 'Explicate'.

'I was watching Madeleine the other day as she was hunting, and I was thinking how yucky it was to have to clean her kills off the doormat. Then I realized that she brought them as an offering to me: like, "I'm a useful cat. See what I did"?'

Martin was looking a little dazed by my excursion into cat psychology.

'So, Jack was an *offering*. Like a dead mouse. "See what I did for you? He gave you a parking ticket, so here he is, delivered to your doorstep".'

'You think someone is in love with Angel and is showing her that by hurting people who upset her?' Martin raised his eyebrows, the picture of skepticism.

'It makes a perverted kind of sense,' I said stoutly. 'And

poor Beverly's purse being put on the hood of Angel's car. To underline the fact that the attack was – in Angel's honor.'

'So, Shelby was hit on the head because he's her husband?'

'Right.'

'Why wasn't he killed?'

'Maybe because I turned on the downstairs light?'

Martin nodded slowly, not as if he was in love with my theory, but to indicate he was giving it consideration.

'But what about Arthur?' he asked. 'That won't wash, with Arthur. I don't think he and Angel have exchanged two words since she moved here.'

'That's where you're wrong,' I said smugly, having that instant figured out where Arthur might tie in. 'Remember, Arthur had called her in to the police station before he questioned me.'

'So this hypothetical admirer just decided he'd given Angel a hard time?'

'I guess. Actually, Faron Henske interviewed her, not Arthur.'

'Angel,' Martin said slowly, doubt in his voice. 'I don't know, Roe. Angel's not the stuff dreams are made of.'

'Not *your* dreams. But I've seen men just about hang their tongues out when she walks down the street,' I said. 'It's because she's so strong and sleek, I expect.'

'Hmmm. That's an interesting theory . . .'

He didn't believe it for a minute.

'And,' I added, having had a few more thoughts, 'the police won't think of it, I bet, because they're seeing this as attacks on two policemen. Beverly could've been mugged and Shelby could've heard a prowler.'

'Roe, the police could be right.'

'Well . . . maybe. But I think I am. I just can't understand,' I added, as I slid the beige-and-gold-enamel barrette into my hair to hold the waves off my face, 'why the police couldn't find the knife Arthur was stabbed with.'

'They certainly searched us all thoroughly,' Martin said, his voice dry. 'Perry Allison had a pocketknife, but it was perfectly clean. I don't think the wound could have been deep at all, if they suspected a pocketknife could've done it.'

'No blood on anyone . . .'

We shook our heads simultaneously at the opacity of the mystery surrounding the parking-lot stabbing of Arthur Smith, police detective.

Martin gave me a kiss and left to go to the hospital, and I finished preparing for church.

As I started a load of clothes in the washer on my way out the door, I reflected that this had been the best morning Martin and I had had in a while; longer than I liked to count up. For the past few months, Martin had been traveling more, had stayed in the office longer hours, had never let more than a day pass without going into the plant. Outside of work hours, the Athletic Club took up more time, and the meetings of all the boards and clubs he'd been asked to join – Community Charity Concern, Rotary, and so on and so on – ate into his lunchtimes and his evenings. I'd been increasingly on my own or thrown into the company of Angel and Shelby, with whom I had little in common, fond as I was of both of them.

As I retrieved my car keys from the hook by the south

kitchen door, I realized Martin and I hadn't gone out together at night, except for four community functions, in maybe three months.

This was not the life the young wife of a handsome, older, wealthy man was supposed to lead, right? He should be hitting all the nightspots flaunting me, right?

I'd heard the stupid phrase 'trophy wife' behind my back on more than one occasion, and I thought it offensive and absurd. Of course I was quite a bit younger than Martin, and I was his second wife; but I was no voluptuous bimbo who'd married Martin for money and security. When Martin wanted to establish himself as the alpha male, he tended to challenge another man to racquetball rather than encourage me to wear low-cut dresses.

It might seem – to an outsider – that Martin, to some extent, had lost his taste for me. That our honeymoon was so far over that I was housekeeper and occasional companion to Martin, only. That I'd gone back to work because I was bored and unfulfilled as a full-time wife. Or that my married life was sterile because I'd found out I was.

Well, I'd certainly succeeded in ruining my morning, all by myself.

I yanked open the garage door and backed out my lowly car, blotting my tears and listening to country and western music all the way to St James's. I pulled into the parking lot at nine-thirty on the dot. Aubrey, our rector, to whom I'd once been nearly engaged, conducted another service in a nearby town at eleven, so we were his early Eucharist.

My eyes were still red, but I powdered over my makeup again to look passable. I could hear the organ playing, so I stuffed my handkerchief and compact back into my purse and slid out of my car. As I slammed the door behind me and began trotting to the church, I heard another car door slam and registered that someone else was even later than I.

Standing at the back of the church, I spotted a familiar head of carefully styled Clairol brown hair. My mother and John Queensland were ensconced in their usual pew in front of the pulpit (John had been having hearing difficulties the past two years). Aubrey, the lay reader, the chalice bearer, and two acolytes were already lined up behind the choir for the procession to the altar. Aubrey and I exchanged fleeting smiles as I scooted past to duck into the next-to-the-back pew, which happened to be empty.

I had no sooner pulled down the kneeler and slid to my sore knees, grimacing with the discomfort, than I became aware of a man falling to his knees beside me.

I finished my belated prayer, shot to my feet, grabbed the hymnbook, and began trying to find my place in the song all the rest of the congregation was singing as the procession went down the central aisle. Suddenly, a hymnbook was thrust in front of my face, open to the correct page. I took it automatically and glanced up.

Dryden was looking down at me, his face unreadable, his eyes expressionless behind his heavy glasses. We exchanged a long look, searching on his part, quite blank on mine, since I hadn't a thought in my head as to why Dryden would be here in my church juggling a prayer book with a hymnbook in the Episcopalian shuffle. He did not make the mistake of trying to establish a bogus rapport by sharing the hymn-book; but he pulled another one from the rack and joined in the singing with a great deal of enthusiasm.

Was this man *everywhere?* I couldn't throw a stick without hitting him.

As we were preparing to listen to the First Reading, he whispered, 'I put the Andersons on a plane this morning.'

I nodded curtly and kept my eyes straight forward. I couldn't think of any good reason why I should be the recipient of this information.

'She said to tell you good-bye, that she appreciated you listening.'

I gave him a quelling look, the look I saved for teenage boys cutting up in the library.

It seemed to work pretty well on Dryden, because he sat through the rest of the service in silence, affording me some much-needed peace. I wondered if he would follow me up the aisle to take communion, but he stayed in the pew.

As we pushed the kneeler up after the final 'Amen', Dryden said quietly, 'They're not coming back. After the incident last night, she's too afraid.'

I nodded acknowledgment. People were chatting all around us, and so far we weren't attracting too much attention. I tucked my purse under my arm and opened my mouth to say a firm good-bye.

'I kind of like you,' he said suddenly.

I wondered if the steam coming out of my ears was visible. I took a deep breath to suck my temper back in. 'I don't care,' I said in a low, deadly voice, goaded into absolutely sincere rudeness. I was furious, and I was also terrified that any moment a curious churchgoer would wander up to be introduced.

Luckily, the rest of the congregation was in line to shake hands with Aubrey, all anxious to get out into the beautiful weather and go home to prepare Sunday dinner. They were also providing a welcome cover of conversational buzz.

My mother was talking to Patty Cloud. The detestable Patty was looking absolutely appropriate, as always. By a *remarkable coincidence* Patty had begun attending St James's soon after Mother married John Queensland, who was a lifelong communicant. John was having a back-slapping conversation with one of his golfing cronies.

So I was safe for the moment; but any second now, Mother'd look around and then the questions would begin when she called me later, about why I was sharing a pew with one of the objectionable men she'd met at Bess Burns's house, and what he was saying to me.

'I got the punching bag out of the airplane for you,' was what he was saying.

I gaped at him.

I finally managed to say, 'How did you know?'

'I was watching. With binoculars. From the top of that ridge between the airport and the road. An experiment your reporter friend thought of, huh? Incidentally, we think she's right; that's probably how Jack Burns landed in your yard. In that little plane, all the pilot had to do was lean over, open the passenger's door, bank the plane, and out he went.'

'You were watching,' I said, unable to believe my ears. I recalled my long struggle with the bag going down the hill, the grueling process of getting it into the hangar and up into the plane, how I'd sworn and sweated.

'Yep. That was my job, till my bosses decided Jack's landing in your yard was incidental. After that they withdrew O'Riley and put me watching the Andersons. But I liked watching you better; I never know what you're going to do. Getting that bag down the hill was pretty hard.'

'Then why the *hell* didn't you come help me?'

It was the only thing I could think of to say, and I spun on my heel and stalked off down the aisle, the last to shake Aubrey's hand. He looked surprised at my expression, which must have been a picture. I said goodbye hastily and hurried out to my car, praying Mother wasn't waiting for me in the parking lot. I love my mother, but I just wasn't up to her today.

Somehow Dryden had gotten to his car quicker than I had, and he was pulling out of the parking lot as I unlocked the driver's door. The car felt oppressively warm and damp inside; I stood by the open door for a minute or two to let the atmosphere clear out.

I needed the time myself. I was stunned and shaken by Dryden's revelation. The thought of being watched when I thought myself unobserved gave me the cold creeps and a hot anger. Dryden must be good; I could believe I'd never spotted I was being followed, but I could scarcely believe Sally hadn't suspected.

But then, why on earth would she?

I quickly considered Dryden cast in the role of Angel's crazy admirer. I had to discard him, though only with great reluctance, after a little reasoning. But Dryden hadn't met Angel until he'd come out to the house to 'interview' me.

At least as far as I knew.

Angel's past was largely unknown territory to me. Angel was not a great one for talking about herself. I knew she'd grown up in Florida, that she'd met Shelby when he paid a condolence call to her folks. Shelby had been a Vietnam pal not only of Martin, but also of Angel's much older brother Jimmy Dell. Jimmy Dell had met his Maker after the war and far away from Vietnam, in the mountains of Central America.

Shelby had waited a few years for Angel to grow up, then he'd married her. They'd always been happy together, as far as I could see. Even the day or two Shelby had doubted Angel's pregnancy was his work had not, in the end, disrupted their relationship.

Maybe somewhere along the way she'd met Dryden. Maybe they'd both been acting cleverly the day I introduced them.

But what would have been the point in that?

Oh, this was all so confusing.

I looked at my watch. Martin had had plenty of time to pack up the invalid and take both Youngbloods home. The funeral wasn't until two. I turned the key in the ignition and put the car into drive.

Automatically, I turned toward home as I left the parking lot. But after a block, I realized I really didn't feel like seeing anyone right now. Perhaps I wanted to sulk awhile; maybe roll in a little self-pity. Sometimes I surfaced from my life to look at it in wonderment and irritation and also a certain amount of bafflement. I should have ended up in a house like my mother's, married to someone like Charlie Gorman, a perfectly nice boy I'd dated in high school. Charlie had always made class vice president; he was the salutatorian; he just missed being handsome. He would have been a good father for, say, two little girls; he'd done well in computers since he'd graduated from college. If I'd married Charlie, I would never have known anyone who died of murder; I would never have seen a dead person. We'd go to Walt Disney World, I dreamed, and we'd camp out . . .

Well, maybe that was going a little far.

But I still didn't feel like seeing anyone I knew, just at the moment.

I went where I often go when human companionship seems undesirable: to the Lawrenceton cemetery. I always park by my great-grandmother.

A narrow gravel driveway makes a figure eight inside the cemetery fence, to allow for parking at funerals and for easier access to the graves. My great-grandmother is one of the few people buried between the encircling driveway and the fence. She was from a farming family; maybe she wanted to be close to the surrounding fields.

Shady Rest is an old cemetery, maintained by a coalition of Lawrenceton's white churches. The segregation of death is much stricter than segregation is in life, now. The black cemetery, Mount Zion, is on the southern edge of town, while Shady Rest is a little out in the country on the west.

Shady Rest is a very ordinary cemetery, traditional, none of this flush-with-the-lawn marker stuff. The earliest tombstones date about twenty years before the Civil War, when Lawrenceton became more than a tiny settlement. There are live oaks and other hardwoods; there is close-clipped grass covering the gently rolling ground. Tiny iron fences interrupted by little gates surround some of the older family plots. There is a high, fancy, ironwork fence enclosing the whole cemetery; but there is no gate to close over the main entrance, though the two other back entrances are gated and usually locked, except during a funeral. There has never been vandalism at Shady Rest, though I'm sure some day there will be. Every now and then, someone donates a cement bench to sit beside one of the two narrow drives that cross through the graves, though I don't believe I've ever seen anyone sit on them but me.

After nodding to my great-grandmother, I go sit by Mr Early Lawrence, most times. Naturally, he was the man Lawrenceton was named after, and he earned it by hustle; an early entrepreneur, was Mr Early Lawrence. Though his descendants don't like to talk about it, somehow Early held on to his money and increased it after the War. Even today, none of the Lawrences are poor folks.

Early Lawrence had a magnificent tombstone, perhaps ten feet tall because it was topped with a stone angel whose hands were outstretched, palms up, pleading – perhaps urging passersby to feel sorry for Early? To remember to mow the grass? I had never quite understood that beseeching gesture, and I often pondered it when more immediate things gave me pain or anxiety.

After the heavy rain of the morning, the ground was soggy. I pulled out the old towel I kept in the trunk of my car, since the bench had a damp look. I picked my way to my chosen spot, spread my flowered towel, and sat down with a sigh.

Close to the center of the cemetery, the green tent was set up over the hole dug to receive Jack Burns, I noted approvingly; Jasper Funeral Home was on the ball. The chairs for the family were unfolded and ready with green covers slipped on. Artificial turf discreetly covered the mound of dirt at the back of the tent. The artificial green was gleaming with water droplets.

I wandered over to have a closer look, and found that the

lowering device was in place over the grave, the green webbing stretched across to receive the casket. I wondered which of the levers on the side released the webbing to let the casket descend, but I was certainly not about to experiment. Sheer interest in the mechanism kept me there for a few moments, until I recollected that into this hole would descend the body of a man I knew, and I beat, a shamefaced retreat to Early Lawrence.

I looked up at the angel, again studying that calm face for some trace of a clue as to its intent. I wondered who had sculpted it; did he churn them out, or make each one as it was commissioned? He'd enjoyed doing the wings, I could tell . . . they were full and beautiful, as feathery as stone could look.

I thought the usual thoughts – what would they say, all these dead Lawrencetonians, if they could see the town now, look over the horizon and see Atlanta approaching, encroaching? What if my maternal grandmother, whom I could faintly remember (she was over there close to Great-grandmother, but within the driveway), could give judgment on her daughter's successes and her grandaughter's peculiar life?

We were not a fertile family; I was the only child of an only child, and according to the specialist, I could not even have that one my mother and grandmother had been granted. I'd known now for two months; but sometimes I still cried when I thought about it. I had to get over that. I began counting my breaths, slow and even; in, out, one, two, three, four . . . self-pity was a drug. I must not become addicted. Self-pity is like chocolate; as you get older, you can only afford a little bit.

I heard a robin, then a mockingbird. Bees did their thing among all the flowering bushes and a few premature Easter lilies, set by gravestones. Here and there was a red foil-covered pot filled with shriveled remains of poinsettias, but on the whole folks took better care of their dead than that.

So peaceful. I deliberately took off my watch and dropped it in my purse. After a while, my tears dried and I cut loose from my worries, letting my mind drift. It was as though the countless religious ceremonies held here had drenched the soil not with anguish, but with calm detachment, thoughts of eternity. Every now and then I'd see a car go by; Shady Rest was perilously close to one of the new housing developments.

When at last I rose I'd achieved peace, or at least calm.

I really wouldn't have had Charlie Gorman on a platter.

I was making my way back to my car, taking my time and reading headstones, when I actually began to think. It seemed to me I hadn't been asking the right questions. I'd been asking *why* these bizarre things were happening, *who* could be doing them, instead of *how*.

I was convinced that all the events of the past couple of weeks were related: the murders of Jack Burns and Beverly Rillington, the murderous attacks on Shelby and Arthur Smith.

Jack Burns had been dumped from an airplane, so the killer had to know how to fly. Jack had been killed by a blow to the head (last night's local paper had said), as had Beverly Rillington, so the killer was strong and not afraid of violence.

Since somehow the killer had approached Shelby, who

still had no memory of the attack, either (for convenience's sake I'd term the killer male) he was someone known to Shelby, someone Shelby had no reason to fear; or he was used to stealth.

And if the stabbing of Arthur in the middle of a crowd was any indication, this person was getting increasingly reckless. The stabbing had to have been impulsive; the weapon was probably a lowly pocketknife, if the gossip I'd heard had been correct. So someone in the crowd around Arthur had been overwhelmed with fury so sudden and devastating that he'd risked all to injure Arthur.

And somehow, somewhere, he'd concealed the weapon so that none of the police on the scene had been able to find a trace of it. Could a pocketknife be swallowed? I wondered wildly. We'd all been searched. Where the hell could it be? This was a crucial *how*. How had it been concealed?

It was the sort of puzzle that I eagerly moved on to find the answer to in every fictional mystery I read. I never tried to figure it out myself when I knew the writer would supply the solution in a page or two. But I couldn't flip to the end of the book now . . .

I rolled down the car window, letting the cool breeze toss my hair. I looked at the proper green tent-roof over Jack Burns's grave. On its surface I replayed the banquet's ending.

Martin and I walked out the door, and he took my hand. Arthur and his date were behind us. I remembered how irritated I'd been with Arthur; how he'd eyed me.

And when I remembered that, a little cold trickle started down my spine.

But I ignored it with a great effort of will. I was going to track this memory.

The cool, sweet evening. The parking lot. The little knot of people on the sidewalk. The quiet voices exchanging pleasantries. Jesse Prentiss introducing Verna, a stout sixty-year-old with a narrow mouth and a tight perm, to the anxious Andersons, who wanted only to be gone. Perry asking Jenny Tankersley if she wanted to go to his place for a drink . . . Paul with his hand in his pocket to retrieve his car keys, his date standing with her arms crossed on her chest; probably having circulation problems because her blue jeans were acting as tourniquets. Who else? Marnie Sands, groping in her purse, looking annoyed. I remembered thinking she couldn't find her keys.

We'd moved to the right, facing out into the parking lot, preparing to cross to Martin's Mercedes. The dog and the cat had provided the diversion necessary for the attacker to make up his mind; he'd try for Arthur . . . the idea of what extreme anger must be necessary to prompt such risk-taking made me shiver.

Then, of course, my fall to the pavement. I touched my bruised face; I had a blue bump on my right forehead, and a little scrape on my right cheek. I'd been lucky.

The confusion, the screaming, the moan and curse from Arthur. Martin helping me up, trying to find out where I'd been hurt. Jesse Prentiss, unexpectedly authoritative, telling Perry to run inside to call the ambulance . . . the sound of Perry taking off. There'd been running feet to and from the scene on the sidewalk: Dryden had run up to us, and Perry had run away.

Paul Allison had said, too late, that he'd called it in from his car already; Perry had been in the building by the time Paul had told us. Perry had had a perfect opportunity to get rid of the knife.

Okay, what about Dryden? His presence at the end of the parking lot was explainable; he was guarding the Andersons. But could he have thrown a knife, somehow? No, I decided reluctantly. Arthur had been facing Dryden's car, and the wound had been in the back of Arthur's shoulder.

Arthur's date, the little gal with the ponytail? Nope. Not only did it not ring true, but she'd been searched. So had Deena Cotton, who hadn't been carrying a purse; and if she'd had a gnat in the pocket of those jeans, I would've been able to count its legs. Jesse and Verna Prentiss had been standing too far away to reach Arthur, by any stretch of their arms or my imagination. Martin and I had been holding hands and had been in front of Arthur. Marnie Sands had been in the right position and had had her hand in her huge shoulder bag . . . but how could she have gotten through the search?

Paul had watched us every minute until his fellow officers had arrived, unless . . . yes, there'd been the seconds he'd knelt beside Arthur, his hand supporting Arthur's head; he'd been staring down at his wounded colleague. There'd been seconds, then.

But as I'd left the community center, I'd seen the police officers examining the area where Arthur had been stabbed. If the knife had been there – and it could only have been concealed hastily – they would've found it.

No. Somehow, some way, Perry had concealed the knife on his way into the community center. Had to be Perry.

I thought of my friend Sally, about how cheerful she'd

been the day we took the punching bag to the airport. She'd already been through so much with Perry, his bouts with depression and his run-in with drugs; the prospect of Jenny Tankersley as a daughter-in-law had to look like Easy Street in comparison. It was inescapable, though, that Perry looked like the best bet for this series of horrible events. He'd looked at Angel with wanting eyes; he'd had a chance to hide the knife.

But that wasn't enough, even close to enough, evidence for an arrest.

I started the car and drove out of the cemetery slowly, not having the slightest idea of where I was going. It was noon, lunchtime. I bought a sandwich from our local barbecue place and ate it sitting in the car, a practice I normally detest. Maybe I should have called Martin. I thought of doing it, then I remembered the day before when I'd had to track him down, and I childishly thought it might do him good to wonder where *I* was for a while. But those were surface thoughts, ideas that just skated through the front of my brain.

I had the feeling you get when everyone begins roaring with laughter at a joke, and you sit anxiously waiting for the punch line to make sense. There was something big and obvious right in front of me, and I couldn't see it. It was like there was a hole in my glasses. In that spot, I was blind, though I could see clearly all around it.

Chapter Ten

I surprised myself by driving to the hospital and asking to see Arthur.

'He's got a police officer stationed outside his room, you'll have to ask her,' said the stout, elderly volunteer at the information desk. So I trudged through the uncomfortably familiar corridors, thinking that if this kept up, I might even learn the floor plan and figure out the reasoning behind it.

Arthur was in a room at the end of the hall so visitors could be seen coming for a long time. The officer in blue outside Arthur's room was indeed a woman, husky and tough in her uniform. 'C. Turlock' said her little name pin, and it seemed an unpromising sort of name.

Sure enough, Officer Turlock was determined to be the snarlingest watchdog a wounded fellow officer ever had, and she found me highly suspicious. Since my head was approximately as high as her elbow, and I offered to leave my purse out in the hall with her, I couldn't see the source of her suspicions – did she think my glasses concealed a hidden dagger?

If Arthur himself hadn't called out to C. Turlock to find out what she was in a lather about, I would have had to give up; but when he found out who was at the door, he ordered C. Turlock to let me in.

Arthur had one of those horrible gowns on. I could see the bandage at the back of his shoulder, where the material had pulled to one side. He looked as if he was in pain; and I was reminded that being stabbed, even with a pocketknife, is a very unpleasant experience.

I stood beside him, looking at him and wondering what to say. He looked right back.

'So, did Perry do it and drop the knife in a garbage can inside the building?' I asked finally.

Arthur's face went through the most amazing changes. First he looked stunned, then aghast, and at last he started laughing. It was a big laugh, from the belly, and C. Turlock stuck her head in to see what was so funny. Arthur made an imperious sweeping motion with his right hand, and she hastily shut the door.

That right hand kept on traveling and grasped mine, drawing me nearer to the bed. I looked steadily into the pale blue eyes that had once turned my legs to jelly.

'I should never have left you and married Lynn,' Arthur said.

'Yes, you should,' I said briskly. 'And you ought to go back to her now, if she'll have you.'

'Can't I detach you from that shady bastard you married?' Arthur's voice was light, but he was serious.

All the troubles Martin and I had flashed through my mind. I shrugged. 'Not with a crowbar,' I answered.

'I don't think Perry did it,' he said, after a moment, dropping my hand.

'Why?'

'Faron Henske hand-searched the garbage cans along the way to the office where Perry placed the call to 911,' Arthur said. 'He looked down drains. He took apart a sink. Faron isn't a ball of fire, but he's a very reliable searcher. And there were cleaning people still in the community center, plus a few guests who stayed to talk or take down some of the decorations, and they say Perry didn't stop on his way to the office.'

'And the office was taken apart.'

'Yes. Of course.' Arthur leaned back against his pillow; I'd only seen him look this bad once before, when I'd nursed him through a bout of flu.

'I'm real sorry you got hurt,' I said.

'I'm real sorry I fell on you,' he answered politely. 'Took you down to the ground, Paul says. Of course, it made the fall easier on *me*.' A shadow of his hard grin was on his face. 'Did you get hurt?'

He sounded rather as if he hoped I had.

'Just some bruises and scrapes.' I pulled back my hair to show him the bump on my forehead.

'Next time I'll try to fall on someone bigger, and land on her front and not her back,' he told me, trying for bawdy.

'Lynn's bigger than me.'

'Roe . . .'

'Okay, sorry. I don't know what went on with your marriage. But I'm not the escape hatch. I'll always have good memories of you, and I don't want them to get sour.'

'Straight from the hip, Roe.'

'Had to be,' I said.

'I love you.' Suddenly he looked twenty, vulnerable and yearning.

'You love what you remember. But you were screwing Lynn on the side for the last three or four months we were together. So I'd say your love wasn't ever an exclusive item.'

'Let me have it when I'm down.'

'Only time I can get you to listen.'

The corners of his mouth twitched in a smile. 'Okay, okay. You listen now,' and he reached for my hand again. 'You take care, Roe. I know you love Bartell, but since you told me what you think about my marriage, I'll tell you what I think about yours.'

Oh, boy, I didn't want to hear this.

'That guy is out of your league, Roe. He's tough and he's ruthless. He's a lot older. He'll never think you're his equal.'

That seemed a very strange charge to level at Martin, and I looked at Arthur in some surprise. I'd been scared, perhaps, that Arthur would tell me he'd kept Martin under surveillance and that Martin had a mistress. Or that Martin was engaged in some criminal activity. Arthur would just love to catch Martin in those situations, and he'd make sure I knew, because he'd warned me from the time I met Martin that I shouldn't marry him.

If Arthur hadn't caught him, Martin wasn't doing it, I suddenly realized. I hadn't known how worried I'd been until the relief spreading through my body made me giddy with cheer.

'I don't know if he thinks I'm his equal,' I said. 'We're so different I think "equal" would be hard to pin down. But he lets me be myself, and he's never tried to change me, and we enjoy each other very much.'

We looked at each other steadily. I thought of how wounded I'd felt at Arthur and Lynn's wedding, how betrayed. It seemed strange now, as though those emotions had been felt by some other person and only told to me.

'Good-bye, Arthur. I hope you get out of the hospital soon.'

'Bye, Roe. Thanks for visiting. I know you're curious about what happened. I'll get Paul to keep you filled in.'

I thought about being embarrassed, decided to skip it.

'Thanks. See you,' I said, and walked through the door.

'Officer Turlock,' I said, inclining my head. She nodded back grudgingly. I didn't feel I'd made a friend.

A glance at my watch told me it was almost time for the funeral. I brushed my hair and powdered my nose in one of the chemically scented hospital bathrooms, and drove to Western Hill Baptist Church.

Western Hill was easily the prettiest church in Lawrenceton, a town of many churches. It sat by itself on the top of a rolling hill in, obviously, the (north) western part of town, which consisted mostly of newer suburbs. The church overlooked Lawrenceton, a calm, white-spired presence that everyone enjoyed. Western Hill was landscaped to the nth degree, with flowers, shrubs, and grass that looked clipped with a level. In its rivalry with the larger Antioch Baptist, which actually possessed an indoor swimming pool, Western gained points with its parking lot, which surrounded the church on three sides; no long slog to the car at Western.

And Western was undoubtedly the best place to have a funeral, though I was sure that hadn't crossed Bess Burns's mind when she'd joined the church years before.

The long black hearse was parked at Western's massive front doors, on the semicircular drive that curved across the hill in a graceful arc. This was a driveway used only for ceremonies; Western had provided back entrances and that wonderful parking lot for regular occasions. I used one of those smaller entrances, and wended my way through the day-care corridor to the sanctuary door. In the sanctuary, the ceiling was two stories high, and the walls and ceiling were dazzling white, giving the impression of light and sky. The sun streamed through the high arched windows and flung a bolt of dramatic light across Jack's dark gray coffin, topped with a large casket spray of white gladiolus, resting at the steps up to the altar.

Jack Burns was being buried on a beautiful day.

I had to walk to the back of the church, since I'd entered from the door to the west of the altar area; as I passed, I scanned the row of pallbearers on the left front pew. I knew all of them, from Jack's fellow officers – Paul Allison, Faron Henske, Chief of Police Tom Nash Vernon, Sheriff Padgett Lanier, and (amazingly) Lynn Liggett Smith – to his son, Jack Junior. I scurried by, not particularly wanting to meet the eyes of any of the people on that pew, especially Lynn.

The church was rapidly filling up, and I ducked into the first aisle space I saw, nodding to Sam and Marva Clerrick sitting in the pew behind me. I was closer to the front of the church than I liked to be, but I didn't want to sit on one of the folding chairs that had been lined up in the back. I got settled, tried to stick my purse under the pew, began to slide to my knees and just in time recalled I wasn't in a church with kneelers.

'Almost hit the ground again, didn't you?' murmured a voice in my ear.

I had a moment of sheer rage when I thought the speaker

was Dryden. Was I going to be approached in every church I entered?

But Martin, perfectly appropriate in a quiet suit, sat down in the pew beside me. I took his hand and squeezed it, my heart thudding in a ridiculous way. I was so glad to see him I was in serious danger of crying, and that would have been noticed this early in the proceedings.

'You came anyway,' I whispered, knowing that was obvious but wanting to say it, nonetheless.

He looked at me sideways, and a little smile curved his lips. 'Missed you,' he said.

Then the organ music changed in tone, the funeral director from Jasper's appeared at the front of the church to signal the family had arrived, and Bess Burns and her daughter walked down the aisle as the congregation rose to its feet. In her black, Bess seemed to have lost ten pounds in a few days, and Romney's round face was bare of makeup and stained with tears. I knew Romney well from her teenage days, barely over, when she'd come into the library three or four times a week. It shocked me to see her look so adult.

I hastily revised my carnal thoughts for those more appropriate to the occasion; whatever Maker there was to meet, Jack Burns up yonder in the stainless-steel coffin had seen that Maker face-to-face. No more mysteries left to solve for that detective.

I wondered if the pall-bearing detectives on the front row had thought of that. I could see a slice of all their faces, as they looked to the right as the minister entered his pulpit. Paul was looking pale and resolute, Faron Henske solemn, and Lynn Liggett Smith was just blank. I'd never expected to see a female pallbearer, but I heard Marva hissing to Sam that Jack had specified Lynn in his will. Arthur was supposed to serve, too, but his wound had prevented it; Paul had replaced him.

The coffin remained closed after the minister's address. I could well believe that it had been impossible for the mortician to reconstruct Jack. So instead of viewing the deceased, a ritual I was glad to forgo, we all retreated to our cars and drove to Shady Rest. Though parking space at Shady Rest would be at a premium, I took my own car and Martin took his Mercedes; I didn't want to leave my Chevette at Western Hill, which was not exactly on the way home.

Martin and I stood in the sun, our heels sinking into the rain-softened ground, while the brief graveside service came to an end. The pallbearers laid their boutonnieres on the casket, and the minister, reminded by their action, did likewise.

The funeral director, a trim blond man I'd never met, bent down to Bess and murmured something, and Bess, wakening from her thoughts, nodded and stood. The funeral was officially over.

Immediately, most of the attendees left to resume their regular Sunday afternoon pursuits.

Romney Burns went around saying hello to people she recognized while her mother had a quiet talk with the minister. I introduced Romney to Martin and we talked stiffly about the day and the service. Romney seemed remote, numb; I felt so sorry for her.

Jack Junior stood by himself, facing out over the adjacent field, smoking a cigarette, his expression savagely angry; I thought I would steer clear of Jack Junior, who was obviously in a very volatile state.

Not everyone had noticed this, however. Somehow uncued by Jack's stance, Faron Henske laid a big, brown would-be comforting hand on Jack's shoulder. Jack twitched away, threw down his cigarette, and abruptly lost control. Those of us looking in his direction could see him pop, and a collective wince ran through us.

The minister was pulling out of the main gate. He should have stayed a few minutes longer.

'One of you did it!' Jack shrieked. Those who'd not seen the windup froze in their tracks; and poor Faron looked devastated at having set off this firestorm.

'He wouldn't turn his back on someone he didn't know! One of you did it!'

Martin looked grim and hard. The blond funeral director, closest to the two, was considering whether to intervene; he thought the better of it, and I was sure he was right. The only person who could handle this came striding across the soft ground; Bess, in her black, wrapped her arms around her son and talked quietly in his ear, her eyes dry. Romney, round and sandy as her father had been, stood a few feet away, scared to join them.

The tension seemed to seep out of Jack as we watched, and the few remaining people scattered to reach their cars, trying not to look as if they were hurrying. Jack was crying as Martin and I turned away. I glanced over my shoulder to see Bess, Romney, and her brother make their way to Jack's car, and leave.

I looked sideways at my husband. If there's anything Martin hates worse than watching strangers pour out strong emotion, I have yet to discover it; that's one reason I go to the movies with Sally or Angel. His lips were pressed together, his gaze straight ahead. Martin looked as if he were tempted to say, 'Thanks a lot, Roe,' but was trying to forbear.

'I'm sorry,' I said with a certain bite in my voice, 'for letting you know I wanted you to come.' I could hardly apologize for Jack's behavior. I eyed him cautiously, waiting to see what his mood was.

'How many years will Lawrenceton recall that little scene?' he asked. I relaxed.

'Forever and ever. Do you think Jack Junior was right?'

'Yes,' said Martin after a second. 'Yes, I think he was.'

I thought of the faces around the grave, all of them known, familiar. I shivered in the bright sun, and Martin put his arm around me.

'I have a feeling,' Martin said, looking straight ahead, 'that we haven't exactly been operating on the same wavelength lately.'

That seemed as good a way of putting it as any. I remembered Martin's first wife telling me that Martin was not a man to talk about problems, and I felt he was doing the best he could, considerably better than I had anticipated.

'I've been working a lot of hours, and when I thought about it on the way home from Chicago, I realized I hadn't been seeing you much, lately.'

This was going almost too well.

'I'll try to be at home more,' Martin said briefly, but not without effort. 'I guess I didn't like it when you went back to work without talking to me about it first.'

The shadow of an oak branch tossing in the wind played over Martin's face.

'Possibly,' I said very carefully, 'we should talk to each other a little more.' We looked at each other cautiously and stiffly, like creatures from different planets who basically bore each other good will, but who did not speak the same language to explain that.

After a long pause, Martin nodded in acknowledgment, and we resumed the walk to his car. As we reached the Mercedes, shining whitely against the green carpet of grass, Martin swung me around to face him, gripped both my arms, and to my astonishment leaned me against the car and kissed me thoroughly.

'Well,' I said when I came up for air, 'that was wonderful, but don't you think we really ought to postpone this until we get home?'

'Everyone has left,' Martin said breathlessly, and I saw that that was true, for the most part. On the other side of the cemetery, the group of pallbearers (minus Jack Junior) was deep in conversation by Paul's dark blue Chrysler, and I remembered all of them were police officers with murders to solve.

The funeral home staff had gone to work as soon as the widow had left. The casket was in the ground, the lowering device had been packed up, and the funeral director and another man were shoveling the dirt into place, while a third man loaded the folding chairs into the funeral home van. I knew from past experience that soon the dirt would be mounded, the flowers laid over it, the artificial turf removed. The tent would stay for a day or so. Then that would be gone; the cemetery would return to its slumber.

'I'll see you at the house,' I told Martin, and rested the palm of my hand against his cheek.

As I bumped the Chevette along the gravel road leading out of the main gates of the cemetery, I passed Paul's car. Paul and Lynn were the only ones left of the group that had been there a few moments ago; I raised my hand as I passed, and Lynn responded with a bob of her head, but she didn't stop talking to Paul. Paul's pallor and sharp features had never been more evident. I thought he was suffering from some distress. He had one hand extended, resting on the roof of his car, and that seemed to be the main thing holding him up. He didn't acknowledge me at all by wave or smile, but fixed me in a stare that seemed to pin me like a captured butterfly. I was glad when I was by him and on the road home; I couldn't imagine what he and Lynn could have been discussing that would make him look that distraught. I glanced once in my rearview mirror to see Lynn's car leaving the front gate of the cemetery, turning left instead of right as I had done.

Perhaps Lynn, too, had come to the conclusion that the person who'd attacked Arthur was Perry, Paul's former stepson and now his friend. That would account for the haggard expression on Paul's bony face.

I thought of how upset he'd been last night, when Arthur had been stabbed; I thought of his unexpected choice of female companion, a woman with poor taste and judgment, so different from Sally. And yet, this was the woman whose rump he'd groped in front of me. I felt again that flash of uneasiness. That hadn't really been Paul-like, had it? Paul had always been calm, controlled, and conservative.

He'd sure lost his calm the night before. His voice had

certainly been ragged when he'd told Jesse he'd already radioed to the police station.

I braked and pulled over to the side of the road. Luckily, there was a shoulder; luckily, no one was behind me.

He'd called from his car.

There *was* someone else who'd had a chance to hide a knife. Paul. The detective who'd guarded us till the other officers could get there.

But why? I raised my hands in front of me to cover my face so I could concentrate.

Why would Paul stab Arthur? They'd never liked each other much, but they'd worked together for years without actually harming each other. What could have precipitated . . . ?

Arthur had separated from Lynn recently. So?

And Arthur had shown up at the Pan-Am Agra banquet with an obviously unsuitable date, as, indeed, had Paul. But Arthur had eyed me all during the banquet. My husband had certainly noticed, and if he had, others would have too . . . why would Paul stab Arthur over Arthur's lust for me? It just didn't make sense.

Yes, it did. But it was hard to admit it to myself, because it seemed so bizarre, so ridiculous. It had been in front of me all the time, but I would not see it, I could not see myself as that kind of woman. Angel had suspected it all along: I remembered the look she'd given me the day Paul had deposited Beverly Rillington's purse on her car hood, mistaking it for mine.

Paul had stabbed Arthur because Arthur had 'dated' me for months, openly wanted me again.

Paul had attacked Beverly Rillington because Beverly

threatened me in public, in front of Perry – who had relayed the scene to his former stepfather, uncle, and friend. Beverly's purse was the evidence of Paul's revenge for her slighting me.

Paul had hit Shelby over the head because Shelby was patrolling my yard when Paul wanted to – break in? Stare at my window? Serenade me in the rain with a mandolin?

I slapped myself in the cheek to keep concentrating, to keep from veering away from thoughts that made me sick. I laid my hands on the steering wheel. They were trembling violently. Think, Roe!

Jack Burns, my longtime enemy, a man known to publicly bad-mouth me, a man Paul had to see every day since he was Paul's boss. The first death.

I'd been so fixated on Angel's magnificence, I'd been unable to read the very clear message. Jack Burns, falling out of that airplane, head over heels, to land in my yard. Like the damn cat bringing me the mouse. A trophy.

See what I did for you?

Oh my God. And I'd left Martin at the cemetery with Paul. And in front of this obsessed man, Martin had just laid a kiss on me that had practically singed my hair.

Chapter Eleven

I did the most reckless U-turn ever performed on a country road in Spalding County. I went as fast as I could bring myself to drive, and prayed heartily that this day above all days a county patrolman had set up a speed trap on this remote little road.

Of course that didn't happen.

I had to think, I told myself frantically. I couldn't just drive in there and make everything all right.

I slowed the car as I reached the cemetery. I swerved the Chevette across the road and into the ditch and didn't care if it stayed there till it rotted. It was off the road.

As though my furious parking method hadn't made any noise, I got out quietly and shut the door with great care. My car had entered the ditch a little above the southeast corner of the rectangular cemetery tract. The main gate was in the middle of the long east side, the two auxiliary gates were on the west, opening out onto a rutted dirt track that ran along outside the length of the fence to tie back into the county road forming the eastern boundary of the property.

From this corner, the trees obscured my view, but I could catch a glimpse of gleaming white up close to the north part of the cemetery where Jack had been buried; Martin's Mercedes.

I shivered all over. I forced my brain to work, to plan.

The main gate on the east was too exposed, visible from most places in the cemetery. So I crept along the fence, through the high weeds, and tried not to let the thought of snakes cross my mind. Since church and funeral going had been the designated occasions when I'd dressed that morning, my clothes and shoes were hardly helpful in ditch-slogging or cemetery crawling. The rayon of the beige skirt caught on everything I passed, the low heels of the pumps sank into the wet earth, and my loose hair was collecting a fine assortment of seeds and burrs.

I reached the track at the southwest corner and followed it, ducking low while trying to run, one of the most difficult things I'd ever attempted.

Every three yards or so I'd stop to look and listen; I heard nothing, saw nothing, cursed the trees and bushes I'd thought so beautiful this morning.

I got to the first rear gate.

It was fairly exposed, though if Martin and Paul were still close to Jack's grave, there were several tall plantings and grave markers between them and me. But I dropped to my stomach and crawled. I reached a good vantage point behind one of the few raised vaults in Lawrenceton, and peered from behind it.

My heart sank. Paul's car was indeed still parked parallel to the west fence; I could see only the back of the tent left over Jack's grave, but I could tell the hearse and the funeral home employees were gone.

I sidled up closer, hugging the granite of the vault. I confirmed what I already suspected – there were no other cars. Paul and Martin, alone here.

And me.

Then I saw them. Martin's left side was toward me, his back against the thick trunk of a live oak, and he was looking several degrees whiter than he had when I'd left. His face was set in lines I'd seen only once before. This was how he must've looked in the war, I thought fleetingly.

Paul was standing with his right side to me, his back to his car, and he had a gun in his hand. He was talking to Martin; though I couldn't hear him, I could see his mouth moving, and I saw from the way Martin had his head cocked that he was listening.

No weapon. I had no weapon.

I couldn't run and tackle him; there wasn't enough cover between the vault and where he was standing.

Would he shoot me?

Maybe not; maybe. He was supposed to love me, after all. But what if he did shoot, and his shooting me didn't give Martin enough time to grab him? Neither of us would be saved.

I had to hurt Paul.

And by God, I wanted to.

But I hadn't anything except my hands, and I didn't think they'd do enough damage to stop him long enough.

What if the knife was still in his car? The thought burst on me like a beautiful firework.

After a moment I realized it was a stupid idea, but it was all I had. As I began my approach to his car, slightly to the rear of Paul's peripheral vision, I realized just how dumb it was. But I considered for a second: he'd had to leave it there during the investigation at the community center. He'd had to leave it in there this morning, when he'd been at the police station, presumably; and he'd had to leave it in there for the funeral, because he couldn't withdraw it during the service or later at the cemetery. So our whole salvation depended on whether or not Paul Allison had been too exhausted the night before to withdraw the knife and clean its hiding place.

He'd parked facing south on the little drive, so I had to creep up the passenger side, and pray the door was unlocked. I was afraid to look toward Paul and Martin, afraid that I would see Martin get shot, afraid that if my eyes met Martin's his face would change and Paul would turn to see me. I could hear Paul's voice ranting on and on and I made my way closer, but I shut out what he was saying.

Finally, I had used all the available cover, including Early Lawrence's angel. I had come to a point where I was blocked by graves or trees, and I had to cross the track that made a large figure eight within the cemetery, about at the cross-loop. I took off my shoes so they wouldn't crunch on the gravel, and tried to think light so my feet wouldn't make noise. I risked a glance; I had worked my way so close that I was nearly behind Paul now. Martin's eyes were focused on Paul. I didn't know if he'd seen me or not.

I had to chance it. I took a deep breath and stepped out into the open. I took one step across the gravel, then another, then I could regain the soft grass and walk quickly to the passenger side of the car.

I looked down at the door. I was so desperate that for a minute, my eyes refused to focus.

The door was unlocked.

Praise God, I thought; I gripped the handle. I had to look again now, and I fixed my gaze on Paul's back, trying not to see Martin over his shoulder. It helped that Paul was the taller of the two by a couple of inches. I did not want to see Martin's face, see the knowledge of my presence reflected in it. I willed Martin not to know I was here. And I pressed in the release button with my thumb.

It sounded like an explosion to me, but I knew the sound was small. I stopped breathing, the car door barely open, waiting to see if Paul would turn my way.

He didn't. He kept on talking. I inhaled deliberately. I was light-headed with relief and oxygen deprivation.

Gently, gently, I pulled open the door. So slowly my thumb cramped, I eased it off the release knob. I unclenched my fingers from the handle. I wiggled them for a second or two, trying to restore circulation.

I crouched again, my sore knees protesting at a barely discernible level. The scabs had come off eons ago in the ditch; I could add blood to the list of items staining my skirt.

But I hadn't made that tiny stain on the blue cloth of the car seat. You'd only see it if you were thinking about blood.

Maybe he'd had it covered with the little notepad that was almost on top of it now; maybe he'd jostled the pad when he'd gotten out of the car.

I looked at the police radio longingly; but I had not the slightest idea how to operate it, and I was scared to death someone would radio Paul while I was crouched here beside the car. I looked over the front seat quickly. If the knife was here, it would have to be around this small area.

The quickest and easiest place to hide the knife would have been to slip it in the crack in the seat.

I slid my hand down into the crack, where I could see the tiny stain. I felt stickiness. I felt a hard shape.

The knife was still there.

My fingers examined it with caution; I didn't want to grab the blade. I gripped it and pulled it out. There was old, dark blood staining my fingers; the stickiness I'd felt. I stared at the knife, wishing I had time to be squeamish. There was dried blood on the little blade and on the hilt. Paul had driven it into Arthur as hard as he could.

It was just a little brown pocketknife, with handy attachments.

Unfortunately, the only one of use to me was the blade.

I stood. I had the knife gripped so the blade pointed upward; all the fictional crime I'd read told me that was the way to use it. I should try to come in under his ribs, I recalled.

I worked my way around the car and stood perhaps twelve feet behind Paul. I was curiously indecisive. Should I sneak up and stab him? Should I scream and run headlong over the grass? The nature of the ground, broken by headstones and footstones, pots of flowers, and a toddler's grave heartbreakingly decorated with a tiny baseball mitt, forbade the scream-and-run approach.

So I began to step quietly over the grass, not daring to look at Martin, focusing on the spot low in Paul's back where I would drive in the knife.

My bare feet made scarcely any sound, and Paul was still talking.

'You've never valued her enough, you can't give her the devotion she needs,' he was telling Martin. 'You go out of town all the time and leave her alone. A husband should stay with his wife. Leaving her with the hired help, you see now that couldn't work! And you let people hurt her. If you really loved Aurora, you wouldn't let these people hurt her!'

I was absolutely determined to kill this man and save Martin's life, but now that I was close to him, I realized I should have run full-tilt after all. This creeping, this planning, was making my soul sick. I could feel sweat pop out on my forehead. My hands were shaking.

I was a yard behind Paul now, and I registered the fact that he'd taken off his suit coat after the funeral – one less layer to penetrate. This was so much harder than I'd ever imagined.

I bit down on my lip, took the last step. My left hand went up to grip his shoulder as my right hand drew back, then plunged in the knife.

Paul made a horrible sound, and his shirt became reddened in a widening circle. I let go of the knife and jumped back to be out of his way when he fell, and he said, 'Walk around where I can see you or I'll shoot him this second.'

I wanted to throw up.

I'd done it. I'd stabbed a man I knew. And there he stood, not falling, not defeated. I did as he said, though my legs were trembling so much I didn't think I'd make it.

The knife, so much heavier at the handle than the blade, slid out of the wound and fell to the ground. I made a horrible noise, but not as horrible as the sound of that knife meeting the dirt.

For the first time I met Martin's eyes. His face was unreadable. He might have been made of stone.

Paul's face was more open. He'd been pouring himself out to Martin, and he hadn't closed the emotional doors yet. He was anguished when he saw his attacker was me.

'Oh, Aurora, how could you do this?' he said wonderingly.

I was so shaken, I found myself on the verge of apologizing.

'You have to spare Martin,' I said to him, willing him to be swallowed up in my intensity.

'Look over there, Aurora,' Paul said gently. 'See the bed of flowers I've got for you?'

The 'bed of flowers' was the funeral arrangements spread neatly on the freshly turned dirt.

'I'll kill him and we'll share the bed of flowers. You deserve something that beautiful, that fragile. You're so beautiful and fragile yourself.'

I shook my head hopelessly, not knowing what to say. Paul was crazy, but not so crazy he couldn't function in his job. I didn't think I could deceive him, since a large part of his work lay in detecting deception.

'Paul, I am willing to go with you if you'll let Martin go,' I said. The seepage of blood had slowed, but not stopped. I felt as if a dog had ripped me up and left pieces of me all over the clipped green grass. I felt the tears beginning to flow. I might not be able to save my husband or myself. I had one more chance.

I held out my arms to Paul Allison and I stepped a little closer. 'Paul, listen, you're – I'm so sorry,' and I began to cry in earnest, but I didn't cover my face, didn't let my arms drop.

'You have to stay where you are, honey,' said Paul. His voice was faltering. 'Please don't cry.'

'No,' I said, and kept on moving slowly, inch by inch, until I wrapped my arms around Paul, holding his to his sides. I laid my head against his chest; how strange it felt to be holding someone built differently from Martin; taller, thinner, less muscled. I could feel Paul's heart beating beneath my cheek. I had sunk a knife into this man's body. His blood was staining my left arm and hand.

And I felt his extended forearm fall to his side, the arm holding the gun. I heard the thud as the gun fell to the grass. I felt both his arms circling me, pulling me closer to him for the first and last time.

He buried his face in my hair.

'Sweet,' he said, and then Martin clipped him in the head with the gun butt.

We had a hard time getting ourselves believed, even after Lynn told the other cops that Paul, his heart overflowing under the emotional pressure of the funeral, had confided in her that day, following Jack's interment, that he was 'deeply involved' with me. He also told her some of the same points he'd raised against Martin: that Martin was an absentee husband, that Martin permitted slander against my name.

To say the least, Lynn was highly skeptical and dubious about all Paul's fantasies. And she knew me well enough to know that's just what they were.

But she wasn't happy to testify against a fellow officer. No one on the police force was delighted to be told that one of their number had murdered another officer, one female civilian, and attacked a male officer and a male civilian.

And Paul popped back into a more rational frame of mind to deny everything except that he had a real crush on me, not exactly an unknown situation. He said that Martin and I had attacked him unprovoked, that I'd misunderstood certain things he'd told me, and that Martin had then pulled Paul's gun from Paul's holster and hit him with it.

That was not exactly a sturdy defense, no matter how much the police wanted to believe one of their own. And there were stains matching Arthur's blood between the seat cushions of Paul's car. And there was a matching stain left on the handle, a stain not washed off by Paul's own blood. Then Jenny Tankersley, that tough flier, came forward to tell Lynn that she'd seen Paul practicing sharp banking moves in one of the small planes she rented, and that she'd noticed something odd: he was opening the passenger door of the little plane while he was flying, then banking to let the door slam shut.

'I knew it was someone after you,' Angel said one day, the day Paul finally confessed to Jack's murder.

'You did?' I said. 'Sure.'

'You thought it was me, but I knew it was you. You just weren't looking at it straight.'

'You seem much more a candidate for obsessive love than I,' I said stiffly.

'It's not your fault,' she said, shading her eyes against the sun. We were lying in our swimming suits on the sundeck, cold drinks at hand. I was trying desperately to feel as lighthearted as the day and the frivolous occupation should have made me. There was not a cloud in the sky. I glistened with oil as though I were going to be fried. I hadn't tried to get a tan in years, avoided the sun as I would the plague. And yet here I was, trying to lighten up my life.

Angel was lying on her back, and I stole a glimpse at her stomach. It was definitely convex.

'That's not *my* fault,' she said.

I closed my eyes and felt myself flushing.

'You gotta work that through, Roe. Or you'll go crazy. There are pregnant women everywhere.'

I nodded. I hoped she was watching.

'You know when the baby comes, Shelby and I gotta find somewhere else to live.'

'I figured,' I said quietly. I turned over on my stomach and buried my face in my arms.

'In fact, before. Because my mom told me after it comes, I'll be too busy to move.'

'So, have you looked at houses?'

'No. I want you to go with me.'

I pushed up on my elbows to look at her.

'Shelby found us this place. I want to find the next one,' she explained, as if every couple operated this way. 'But I've never bought a house, I don't know what to ask or look for, and you do. Will you come with me?'

'Sure.' I was glad I had on dark glasses.

Actually, I could call my mother and she could be on the lookout. They'd need at least three bedrooms; maybe they'd have another baby . . . or Angel's mom might come to help take care of this one . . . and they'd want a yard for the child to play in. I projected Shelby's income and I ran through the neighborhoods in Lawrenceton that would suit it.

'Would you want a pool?' I asked.

I saw Angel's mouth curve in her slow rare smile. 'Sure,' she said. 'Gotta get our exercise somehow.'

A shadow fell across Angel's legs.

'Martin!' I said in amazement. 'You're back early.'

'I told them they didn't really need me at that meeting. They could have asked me everything they needed to know on the phone,' he said, setting his leather briefcase down on the deck and loosening the knot of his tie, an act I never failed to find sexy.

Lately I'd been finding precious little sexy, and I hadn't been able to go back to the cemetery. I had a feeling I'd never sit there in peace again.

Angel said suddenly, 'I'm done to a crisp, and the doctor told me not to get too hot!' She gathered up her towel and lotion and strode off to her apartment without further ado. I heard her tromp up the stairs, and just a few seconds later, tromp down again. 'Gotta go to the store!' she yelled.

Surely that was a little peculiar?

I opened my eyes. Martin had taken off his starched white shirt, his shoes and socks, and was slipping down his pants.

'Good Lord!' I exclaimed.

'No, just me,' he said.

'Did you give Angel some signal?'

'Yes, this.' And Martin pointed at the chaise where Angel had been baking, pointed to the garage, and made a pantomime of hands on the steering wheel.

'What! Why?'

'Because I want to have sex with you on our sun-deck right here and now and I don't want Angel to watch,' Martin said.

'Oh.'

'Because you haven't seemed to want to do that lately, and I thought maybe an exotic locale would – stimulate your interest,' Martin continued, stimulating my interest right then and there, in front of God and the big blue sky.

'Martin! Don't do that!'

'Why not?'

'Well . . . I don't know . . .'

'Then why don't I do it a little longer?'

'Ahhh . . . okay.'

'Then maybe I could just move this chaise over by yours . . .'

'Oh. Urnhmm. And then?'

'I was thinking you could show me how you put that oil all over . . .'

'And then?'

'Roe, I may be too old for a "then"!'

'Oh, not you,' I said confidently.

And I was right.

Acknowledgments

I'd like to acknowledge the fact that Joan Hess gave me exactly one suggestion for this book when I was in a bind; and give thanks for a most informative morning spent with Jackie Cranford. But most of all, I'd like to give credit or blame to Dean James, who thought of the title for this book over a margarita in Austin, Texas.

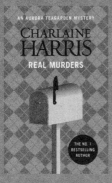

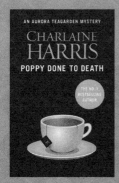